P9-EMC-769

Christie took hold of the door handle — it felt strangely cold as she undid the latch. The door slid open, and as she stepped inside, she was swallowed up in blackness. She turned the barn lights on. Prince stood in the center of the stall, facing her, waiting for her. She picked up his brush and moved to him. He stood calmly, somehow larger, his coat ebony and glistening. Dark shadows arched around him to the rafters overhead. Then the shadows closed in on Christie and she felt another presence.

A low laugh seemed to come from the shifting shadows. Was that a man standing in the dark watching her, a man dressed in animal skins, something glittering on his chest? No, it must be shadows.

She felt happier as she stroked Prince. But behind the happiness lurked a strange, confusing fear. She knew what she felt was unnatural, forbidden. And someone was watching, waiting with terrible sureness for her to take another step into the unknown.

Voices in the Dark

JAMES HAYNES

TWILIGHT™

WHERE DARKNESS BEGINS...

Chapter One

Christie Moncrieff stood with one foot on the locker room bench where she had been tying her shoe. They were talking about her. She recognized one voice as Sue Ellen Lindsay's and thought the other might belong to Jana Wells.

"I think Christie Moncrieff is a real snob." The voice was Sue Ellen's.

"Just because her mother's a writer and she's from someplace near Chicago, she thinks she's a big deal," responded the voice Christie thought was Jana's. "She even says her dad's a grain broker instead of a salesman."

"My dad's a farmer, my grandfather was a farmer, and I'm proud of it. We don't need someone new coming into Herbert Hoover High and looking down at us." It was Sue Ellen again.

Christie went cold. Why were they saying those horrible things about her? She had tried to be friends. She wanted so badly to fit in. She moved to Bethel, Iowa, from Glen Ellyn, Illinois, in late August. Ever since school started, she had done everything she could think of to make friends. But it wasn't easy in a small town where all the kids had grown up together.

"She thought it was a big deal to get everyone to go to that Kansas rock concert over in Ames, too. She just wanted to boss people around." It was Jana's voice again.

"Right. We're all supposed to like what she likes. Are you ready?"

"Yes, let's go."

Christie heard their footsteps fade as they left the locker room. She stuffed the rest of her gym clothes into the locker and closed it. She leaned against the door as tears welled up in her eyes. She tried so hard. Where had she gone wrong?

As soon as she got home from school Christie went down to the barn, saddled her horse, and took him out for training. Riding Prince always helped get her mind off her problems. As far as she was concerned, the Arabian colt was the only good thing about the move to this no-man's-land. Although she knew that he had been a bribe from her parents to help her face moving, Christie adored Prince and found comfort in him.

The physical exhilaration of riding a horse helped to ease Christie's unhappiness. Ever since she was a baby she'd had an almost mystical attraction to horses. She'd tried to climb up on a policeman's stallion when she was only two.

Her parents sent Christie to a riding academy as soon as she was old enough. Even then, the instructor insisted that she must have had lessons before. She didn't show the slightest fear of the huge animals and seemed to know instinctively how to ride. During summer visits to her grandfather's farm she rode the farm horses so professionally that her parents joked that she made them look like thoroughbreds.

During one visit as she helped her grandfather clean out the barn, she felt a slight shock as her fingers uncovered a tarnished, twisted piece of metal. An odd sensation tingled through her body.

"What's this?" she asked.

Her grandfather took the object, and he too flinched as a tiny shock stung him. He turned the metal over in his hands.

"I remember this," he said. "It's an old horse brass. An ornament. My father used to put it on the harness of Star, the black horse that pulled our buggy when I was a little boy. He said our ancestors brought it with them from Scotland. I haven't seen it in years. Look, there's a picture on it under all that dirt."

Christie peered at the ancient piece of metal, but all she could make out under the grime of the years was the outline of some sort of figure. Her grandfather smiled.

"My father—your great-grandfather—was a fine horseman and a wise man," he said. "I remember something he always used to say when things went wrong on the farm: 'Never wish for anything—you might get it.'"

He shook his head and frowned for a moment. Then he looked at Christie, his eyes twinkling. "Here, honey," he said. "Take this and save it until you have a horse of your own. You can straighten it out and polish it up and hang it to jingle on his bridle."

Christie was delighted to accept the old horse brass. As the years passed, it seemed that growing up in the city she wasn't likely to own a horse. She put the ornament in a drawer and forgot it until she was packing for the move to the farm. Cleaning out her bureau, she touched something that gave her a familiar shock. Christie was thrilled to find the brass. She took the ornament to the kitchen and shined it with silver polish. It was badly bent, but with a hammer and patience she managed to straighten it until the figure stood out clearly. It was an unrecognizable, repulsive animal—ugly, but somehow fascinating to Christie.

As she stared at the strange beast, Christie felt the kitchen suddenly grow colder. She shivered and was overcome by a sensation that someone was in the room with her. She turned around quickly, but she was alone.

It must be my grandfather's spirit, she thought, trying to laugh off her uneasiness. He wants me to use this old horse brass and came to make sure that I fixed it. She liked the idea, silly as it was. When she moved to Bethel, she attached the brass ornament to her new horse's bridle. It shone like gold now as she and Prince trotted around the field.

She put Prince into a canter and started doing figure eights from one end of the practice lot to the other. It felt good to ride through the warm autumn air, but Christie couldn't forget the conversation she'd overheard.

Everything had been great back home. She'd had loads of friends, she was president of the sophomore class, and an assistant editor on the school newspaper. Best of all, she'd been going out with Robbie Cranston, the captain of the soccer team. Why did it all have to change?

When her grandfather died he left a will which left Christie and her parents the farm—but only if they came to live on it. He wanted to keep it in the family, as it had been for generations. Her parents accepted his wishes. Before Christie knew what was happening, it had all been decided.

Christie had loved visiting the farm at Christmas and Thanksgiving when her grandfather was still alive. But living there was a completely different story. It was easy for her parents. Her father was a grain broker—no matter what Sue Ellen thought, that's what he was called in Chicago—and out here with all the corn and soybeans he was right in his element. Besides, this was his home. Her mother was a writer and found the old white frame farmhouse a quiet place to work. Christie's parents enjoyed living in the country, where people were friendlier and the pace slower than in Chicago. But neither of them realized how hard it was for Christie to make friends. She was so lonely she'd cried every night since the beginning of her junior year at Herbert Hoover High four weeks ago. She felt numb with misery.

When her mother called her for supper, Christie tied Prince's reins to the saddle horn so he could graze while she ate.

"How was your day, sweetheart?" her father asked.

Christie didn't look up from her plate. "Okay," she lied. It wouldn't help to complain. No matter how concerned her folks might be, there was nothing they could do to improve her situation short of moving back to Glen Ellyn. And she knew that wasn't about to happen.

As Christie finished her dinner, her mother looked at her sadly. "You go ahead and take care of Prince, honey. Your father and I will clean up the dishes. Won't we, Roger?"

"Sure thing. Go ahead, Christie."

She was glad to be alone again with Prince. She worked him hard, putting him through his different paces. He seemed to enjoy it. They spent a good hour on jumps, and it was dark by the time they finished. Prince was lathered from the exercise, and Christie was tired. Prince's gentle nicker reminded her that he was hungry. She gave him his evening measure of grain and began to dry him off.

As she listened to the horse crunching his feed, Christie looked around the dark interior of the barn, which seemed distorted by shadows stretching across the wall of fresh hay. The barn seemed much deeper than it really was and gave the impression of sheltering unfathomed secrets.

She couldn't forget the conversation in the

locker room, and she felt so miserable that she could barely hold back her tears. She was so lonely, while everyone else was out having fun.

She folded the towel she had been using to wipe Prince, who sighed softly, bowing his head to take another mouthful of grain from the wooden feedbox.

"Oh, Prince," she murmured. The sound of her own voice in the quiet of the barn startled her for a moment. "I wish you could understand me. I need someone to talk to so badly."

She heard a slight rustling in the darkness. It sounded like a footstep. It's probably just a mouse in the hay, she thought.

Taking Prince by the bridle, she pulled his head down and put her cheek against his. If only things were different. If only wishing made things change! "I wish I had lots of friends and a dark-haired boyfriend like Robbie Cranston. And I wish I could become a fashion designer," she whispered to him. "There, that ought to cover all the bases." She laughed, embarrassed at herself, and the sound echoed back to her from the hollow recesses of the barn. The shadows seemed to deepen in response to her voice. She looked around the barn. Was someone in there with her?

It was getting late and Christie decided to get back to the house. She refilled Prince's water tub and glanced around the stall to make sure everything else was in order. Christie noticed that Prince had knocked down the plastic milk container she'd hung in his stall. He'd played with it, kicking it across the dirt floor until it was flattened. She would have to remember to replace it tomorrow.

Switching off the barn light, she took the flashlight and started for the house. The oak woods smothered her in darkness, as she picked her way down the winding path through the black silhouettes. Christie felt cold, despite the warm September air. The leaves rustled in the blackness overhead, as she directed the flashlight beam on the ground in front of her.

"Criosdan," a voice said, so quiet she could barely hear it. She had never heard the strange word before. But it sounded like her name in another language.

Startled, she turned and flashed the light through the trees. Had it really been a voice, or only the rustle of leaves? She wasn't sure. Why would anyone be hiding in the horse lot to play tricks on her? Their nearest neighbor was half a mile away. Her heart raced at the thought of being watched by someone concealed in the trees. She swallowed and hurried on. At the next bend the house came into view, and Christie felt relieved to see its lighted windows.

She pushed open the gate to the back yard, but hesitated, turning to look back through the woods at the barn. She thought she could see Prince standing in the barn doorway, looking toward her. Quickly, she locked the gate behind her and headed for the house.

"Prince okay?" her father asked as she walked through the front door.

"Sure, he's fine." Christie pushed aside the

weird feeling that had come over her in the barn. In the warmth of her home, she felt foolish she'd let it get her.

That night Christie's sleep was disturbed. In her dream, she was riding across a rocky landscape, seated behind a male rider who wore a jacket of animal skins. Storm clouds rolled low overhead, blocking out the sun and the tops of distant mountains. She felt exultation mingled with terror. She could feel her legs stretched around the broad girth of the horse, the wind whipping past them as they galloped over rough rolling hills. They finally stopped on a high point of ground where she could see her house and Prince's barn below. The images recurred several times, but Christie couldn't make out the rider's face.

Christie thought she heard her name pronounced and awoke with a start. She looked around but could see only shadows. She breathed deeply and rolled over on her side, puzzling over the strange dream. She finally fell asleep as sunlight began to fill the room.

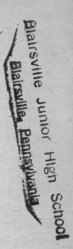

Chapter Two

In the morning Christie felt drained by her restless night. Christie gazed at herself in the mirror. Her face was pretty, but wore a solemn expression.

"I'm not going to make friends looking like that," she told her reflection. "Where's the old Christie spirit?"

She stood up straight, squaring her shoulders, and grinned broadly at herself.

"There," she said. "That's more like me."

Satisfied with what she saw, Christie went down to the kitchen for her morning juice and milk. She knew her mother would nag her about not eating something solid.

11

"Hi, sweetheart!" her dad said, looking at her over his *Des Moines Register*.

"Good morning, dear," her mother said absently. "Eat a good breakfast, now." Her mother listened to news as she made notes on a sheaf of pages, the second draft of her new novel.

"Hi," Christie greeted her parents, trying to keep up her cheerful act. She knew they meant well, even if they couldn't understand what it was like to be a teen-ager.

She finished her milk and juice quickly and hurried out the door. She walked briskly up the long lane to the blacktop road where she caught the school bus. The stocky woman who drove the bus smiled as Christie boarded and made her way to an empty seat near the back.

The first day of school the other passengers had shown a passing interest in Christie. But then the elementary and junior high kids went back to yelling, making fun of each other, and knocking books to the floor. The noise never seemed to bother the driver, but Christie was always glad when the younger kids got off.

The high school students sat in silence through the last mile of the ride. The only sound was the squealing of the brakes as the bus pulled into the semicircular driveway in front of Herbert Hoover High.

What a change from her old school. The thought depressed Christie. She missed the bustle and activity of of Glen Ellyn High. It was great to live only twenty miles from downtown Chicago. There had always been something to do in the city. She and her friends often went to hear popular rock groups in concert.

No such thing in Bethel. It was sixty miles from Des Moines and about the same distance from the state universities at Ames and Iowa City. When Christie first came to Bethel, a few kids paid attention to her, and she talked to them about music—her favorite hobby, next to riding. Some of her classmates seemed to be interested, so she talked them into going to a Kansas concert in Ames. Christie had hoped it would be a good chance to make friends, but the trip had been a disaster.

The kids she'd invited weren't really rock fans, and they spent most of the drive talking about the Bethel football team and how Scott Samson had quarterbacked last year's team to the Class 2A championship held at the University of Northern Iowa. Christie felt left out and tried to change the conversation by mentioning her mother's latest book. Ordinarily, she would have avoided what seemed like bragging, but her eagerness to be included clouded her judgment. Now Christie remembered what Sue Ellen and Jana were saying and she realized her good intentions had backfired.

"Time to get off, dear." Christie jumped as the driver called her from the front of the bus. Christie had been so deep in her own thoughts that she hadn't realized the other students had already gotten off. Embarrassed, she gathered her books and followed them.

*   *   *

"Hi, Goldilocks! Mind if I sit here?"

Surprised, Christie looked up from the fashion magazine she was reading as she ate a tuna sandwich. It was Hal Sloan. He was in her third-period social studies class.

"No, go ahead," she replied.

Hal was tall and slender. He had a friendly smile, and everyone seemed to like him. She knew his friends called him Hawk, probably because of the shape of his nose and the intensity of his deep, dark eyes. The combination made him good looking in an unusual way. He had a rangy build and an air of assurance. Christie knew he was a star on the football team.

"How're ya doing, Goldilocks?"

"Please don't call me Goldilocks." She felt a little angry.

"Sorry." He smiled broadly. "Didn't mean to offend. The name's Christine, isn't it?"

"That's right. Or you can call me Christie."

"I'm Hal, or Hawk, whichever you like best. You're new in school this year. Where are you from?" he asked.

"The Chicago area. Glen Ellyn, to be exact."

"Hey! A big-city girl. What brings you to rural America?"

"My family. When my grandfather died last summer my parents decided to move to his farm."

"Where's your farm?"

"Out north of town near the Izaak Walton Park."

"Oh. Now I've got you. You're one of those Moncrieffs."

"What do you mean, one of those Moncrieffs?"

"Nothing really. It's just that your family's been pretty big stuff around here for years. Your grandpa owned most of the good farm land around these parts. Your dad going to farm?"

"No. He's going to rent out the land like my grandfather did the last few years. My dad's a grain broker and does his business out of his office at the farm."

"Fantastic! Chicago's—or Glen Ellyn's—loss is dear old Bethel's gain."

"That's doubtful." Christie smiled, slightly embarrassed.

"Hey, Rod! Dee! Come on over!" Hawk waved to a couple carrying trays from the meal line. The boy sported a sandy beard and round metal-rimmed glasses, and the girl had staight blond hair that reached her waist.

"Sit down. I want you two to meet Christie Moncrieff. Christie, this is Rod Banners, my driving buddy, and that's Dee Frey. Christie's from Glen Ellyn, near Chicago."

"Hi," Rod and Dee said together.

"Noticed you around," said Dee.

"You fix that tie rod on the Screaming Eagle?" Rod asked Hawk.

"Wasn't the rod. It was a ball joint, and it's fixed."

"What in the world are they talking about?" Christie asked Dee.

15

"Hawk's jeep—it's the love of his life. It's black with a gold eagle on the hood, and he calls it the Screaming Eagle. These guys are big on four-wheel-drive vehicles. They raise the bodies and put oversized tires on them so they can race through fields and ditches without getting hung up. It's Iowa's version of dune-buggy racing—without the sand dunes." She smiled at Christie.

Hawk and Rod went on talking cars while Christie and Dee chatted.

"What are you into?" asked Dee.

"Oh, music, clothes, the usual," replied Christie. Then, hoping to find a mutual interest, she returned the question. "How about you?"

"I like the usual stuff too, especially music. My favorite group is Led Zeppelin."

"Mine, too!" Christie was pleased. "I could listen to them forever."

"That Jimmy Page is something else. Sometimes I think 'Stairway to Heaven' was written just for me. That's crazy, isn't it?"

"It sounds better to me than jeep racing." Christie said, enjoying the conversation.

Dee nodded and called to a girl at a nearby table. "Hey, Lisa! Come on over. I want you to meet someone."

Lisa, a brunette with bangs down to her eyes, walked over. Soon they were joined by two other girls and a boy named Jake. The table where Christie had been sitting alone became wonderfully noisy with conversations about car races, homework, clothes, and music. Christie discovered that these kids had all been at the Kansas

16

concert and never missed a rock show in the area. For the first time since she had come to Bethel, Christie felt she was part of a group. Laughing at their lighthearted kidding, she noticed Hawk watching her. He winked and smiled.

The bell rang, and it was time for afternoon classes. Christie was sorry to leave her new friends. They smiled warmly as they said good-bye to her. Dee turned and said, "We should get together after school one of these days and listen to records."

"I'd love to," Christie answered.

"Wait up," Hawk called to her after Dee left. "You have a way home after school?"

"The bus."

"Want a ride?"

"Sure," she said shyly.

"Good. See you later, then."

That afternoon Christie was joyful for the first time since she'd come to Herbert Hoover High.

Smiling, she walked into her last class of the day. The teacher assigned Scott Samson to be her biology lab partner. Scott smiled a funny sideways grin at Christie's reluctance to dissect their lizard. But he quickly became engrossed in the project, identifying the different organs for her as they were removed. She watched his strong hands move quickly and surely, his pleasant face set in deep concentration. A lock of black hair fell across his forehead. Christie was surprised by a sharp thrill that ran through her at his nearness. He was more attractive than she had thought at first.

Turning her attention back to the lizard, she

17

asked him about a dark round object in its cavity.

Scott looked up, his eyes twinkling. He seemed to be playing a game. "It's a half-digested beetle. Want a bite?"

"Oh, I'm sorry I asked." They laughed, and Christie felt accepted. Scott seemed to like her.

At the end of the day, Hawk met her at the door to the basement locker area.

"Are you ready? I'd like to get moving."

"Just let me get my algebra book. I've got a double assignment over the weekend, and I want to do some studying."

"Brains as well as beauty, eh? I'll meet you out back."

Hawk's jeep was parked in the seniors' parking lot. It was just like Dee described it. A golden eagle, its wings spread as if in flight, was painted across the shiny black hood. The name Screaming Eagle was painted in matching gold script on the doors. Christie admired the jeep's beautiful deep finish, and Hawk smiled proudly.

"It's beautiful." Christie was genuinely impressed.

"She's a she, and beautiful's the way I like all my women," he laughed. Christie flashed him an embarrassed smile.

Hawk started the engine, backed out of the parking place, and stopped at the lot exit to let several students pass. Sue Ellen was among them and seemed surprised to see Christie in the jeep with Hawk. She looked at the pair sharply, then nudged the girl she was walking with and nodded in their direction. The girl raised her eyebrows questioningly, and she and Sue Ellen hurried away.

Christie noticed their exchanged glances and remembered the scene in the locker room. What are they thinking now, she thought. But at that moment Hawk revved up the motor and turned onto the main road.

The ride home in the open Screaming Eagle began pleasantly. The sun warmed Christie, and the fragrant early autumn wind brushed back her hair. But when they reached the edge of town, a big grin spread across Hawk's face. "Hang on," he said, accelerating through a turn onto a gravel road. The Eagle leaned precariously to the left, fishtailing and spraying gravel through the air, before it finally straightened out. Christie was thrown against Hawk's shoulder and clutched her books so they wouldn't fall off the seat.

"Hawk!" she squealed. "Do you have to drive so fast?"

"Only way to fly! You ain't seen nothin' yet."

With those words he whipped the jeep off the road. They sped through an open pasture gate and raced across a field. Christie grabbed for the handholds, letting her books fall to the floor. Her eyes opened wide in alarm as they headed for a row of trees and underbrush that protruded from a gash in the ground directly in front of them. Was he out of his mind? Was he going to crash into the woods? The trees seemed to rush toward them, and Christie squeezed the handholds until her fingers hurt. She started to scream at the expected impact, but at that moment Hawk swerved, and they slid through an opening in the trees that she hadn't been able to see. Suddenly, the Screaming Eagle was heading down into a dry river bed, careening along between banks that were as high as the sides of the jeep. If Hawk made one wrong move, she knew they'd crash.

Christie held her breath as the Eagle danced like a bucking bronco through the ruts and over the rocks left by the water that had created the now-dead stream. Her head whipped back and forth, the turns of the river passing in front of her like a movie at high speed. Oh, please make him stop, she cried to herself, unable to call out. She stared ahead in terror.

Finally, she caught her breath and shouted, "Hawk, stop!"

Almost as if he were waiting for that command, Hawk turned the steering wheel sharply, and the Screaming Eagle lurched up the bank on the left. Arching through the air, the jeep burst through the trees and bounced into another field.

Christie caught her breath as the vehicle slowed. To her surprise they were within a hundred yards of her house. Hawk drove carefully across the field and back onto the blacktop before pulling into her lane.

Christie was completely unnerved. The muscles in her hands ached, and her clothes were damp from fear when the jeep came to a stop in front of her house. She sat still for a minute.

"Hawk, I don't like driving like that. It was scary. Please don't do that again when I'm with you."

"Sorry. I thought you might get a kick out of it. Like riding a roller coaster. I won't do it again. I promise."

His face grew serious. "You going to the game tonight?"

"I hadn't planned to," she said tentatively.

"Why don't you? We'll go to Quick's Drive-In afterward. I promise to drive safely. I'd pick you up, but we've got to be at the stadium an hour and a half before kickoff.

"That sounds like fun. I'll come if I can get a ride from my parents, which shouldn't be a problem. I'll probably see you there."

"I'll be looking for you."

Christie watched as he wheeled the jeep around, sped back up the lane, and turned onto the blacktop without stopping.

Hawk was a little wild, but she liked him. Christie had to admit that he was cute. Of course, she didn't feel the same attraction toward him that she had toward Robbie—would she ever feel it again?—but maybe she and Hawk could be friends.

Then she thought of Scott Samson. As she walked toward the big farmhouse she remembered the way she had felt sitting near him in biology lab. Things change so. It was only yesterday that she had told Prince how lonely she felt—that she wished for new friends, a new boyfriend, and success as a fashion designer someday. Two of the wishes had come true already! But she was being silly. There was no reason to believe that she and Scott would even date. One good day, and she

21

was daydreaming of romance. Still, there might be a chance for something to work out between them.

"I'm home!" Christie called as she pushed open the front door.

"Be right with you," her mother called from her office. Mrs. Moncrieff made it a practice to take a break from her writing each afternoon when Christie came home from school.

Christie was microwaving a burrito for a snack when her mother finally came down the stairs.

"How was your day, dear?" her mother asked.

"Super. Really great, Mom."

"My goodness, you're happy. What a nice change from that glum face you've been wearing."

"I met some really neat people today, and I've got a date for after the game—that is, I do if I can get you or Dad to give me a ride into town about seven o'clock."

"What happened to the old custom of a boy coming to pick up his date? Or is that another practice that went down the drain when I wasn't looking?"

"He's on the football team and has to be there early. He'll bring me home, though."

"At least they still do that." Her mother laughed. "That's the best part of a date, isn't it?"

"Oh, Mom." Christie felt her cheeks color.

"We could have dinner a little early if you like," her mother offered. "I'll start cooking while you take care of Prince."

Christie thanked her mother and changed her clothes before going to the practice lot.

Prince trotted to greet her as she came through

the gate, and led her to the barn, occasionally trotting ahead and turning back as though trying to hurry her on. When they reached the barn, Christie filled his feedbox with grain. Every day Prince picked up burrs in his forelock, which had to be picked out, one by one, during his evening brushing.

"Prince, last night I told you my three wishes. Well, I got two of those today!" Christie stroked the horse affectionately. "Two out of three's not bad, fella, especially for a couple of amateurs like us. Think you could make the last one come true?" She laughed, pulling his head toward her so she could scratch behind his ears. He nickered softly and nudged her with his velvety nose. Absent-mindedly, Christie reached up and touched the ornament on his bridle.

Suddenly, the young horse jumped as though he'd been stung by a bee, and bolted from the barn. Surprised, Christie followed him. Prince stopped about twenty feet from the barn and backed skittishly as she approached.

"Whoa, boy," she soothed. "What's the matter?"

When Christie finally caught hold of his bridle, Prince pulled his head back, trying to avoid her. He rolled back his large brown eyes, exposing the whites, and shook his entire body, obviously very frightened.

"What's wrong, boy? What's gotten into you? No, now settle down," she coaxed.

Suddenly, Christie felt that someone was watching her. She turned quickly, almost losing her hold of Prince's bridle, but no one was there. Trying to shake off the creepy sensation, she tried to calm the horse. But he refused to go back into the barn. Still a little uneasy herself, Christie didn't want to go into the barn either.

"It's okay, boy. You can stay out here while I go to the game," she comforted the animal.

Heading toward the house, Christie paused at the gate and glanced back at Prince. *Still spooked!* He darted to the opposite end of the field. Christie stared at him for a minute, unable to shake the feeling that someone was watching her. In the rustle of the autumn wind blowing through the trees, she thought she heard someone laughing at her—a low, harsh, mocking laugh.

Christie turned and ran to the house.

Chapter Three

The streets near the football stadium were lined with parked cars by the time Christie's father let her off at the main gate. She joined the crowd filing into the stadium. Many of the fans wore gold jackets with the head of a Trojan warrior emblazoned on the back. Some wore black-and-gold baseball caps, and others wore gold sweaters or scarfs to show their team spirit. Christie was dressed in a black turtleneck and a light-yellow sweater. She wished she had something gold to wear and made a mental note to talk to her mother about getting a new sweater.

The man at the gate smiled as he punched her student activity ticket and directed her toward the student seats at the south end of the home stands.

Christie took a program and zigzagged her way through the crowd along the sidelines. When she reached the student section, she scanned the rows for a friendly face and finally spotted Dee. Rod was sitting next to her, talking to the boy behind them.

Dee and Rod must be going together, Christie noted. They make a nice couple.

As Christie climbed the steps, Dee spotted her and waved. "Hi!" she called cheerily.

"Mind if I sit with you?" Christie called, happy to see her new friend.

Dee nodded, moving closer to Rod to make room for Christie.

Christie took the seat and looked down at the gold-and-black-uniformed Trojan players running through their pregame drills at one end of the field. The Macon City players, in red and white, were spread from sideline to sideline at the other end doing calisthenics.

Christie looked at her program and found Scott Samson's name. He was number twelve. She spotted him down on the field, where the Trojans were arranged in two lines, alternately throwing passes to one side and then to the other as players broke downfield.

Hawk's number was eighty-two, and he stood half a head taller than the players around him. When it was his turn, he shot down the field like an arrow. Scott fired a low, hard pass that barely arched, and Hawk reached out and caught the ball without breaking stride.

"That's why Bethel's going to the championship again this year," Dee said enthusiastically. "If all else fails, Scott and Hawk go to work and score some points."

Macon City kicked off to Bethel. The home team was hot. Scott completed short passes to Hawk and handed off to the fullback, who ran up the middle. Sometimes Scott kept the ball himself and was able to skirt the ends for big gains. The Macon City team couldn't stop Bethel's seventy-yard drive, a series of plays that ended on a pass from Scott to Hawk for a touchdown.

After that, nothing could stop them. Bethel, a small school, had many players who played both offense and defense. Scott was one of them. Time after time he tackled runners, got off passes and made end runs. He seemed to be all over the field at once, and Christie thought she heard his name announced over the crackly public-address system after almost every play. He was every inch the standout player she had heard about. And he didn't seem quite as macho as Hawk. Scott was definitely someone special.

The final score was 42 to 0. The Bethel players ran from the field, dancing around and shouting their victory. Looking up into the stands, Hawk caught sight of Christie and Dee and grinned as he raised two fingers in a V sign. Dee waved back at Hawk excitedly as Christie looked around for Scott.

The crowd began to file out of the stadium. "Are you going anyplace?" Dee asked Christie.

"To Quick's Drive-In."

"Super. That's where everyone meets after the game. Do you need a ride?"

"No. I've got one, but thanks anyway."

"Great! I'll see you there."

"Okay. See you."

Christie waited for Hawk at the main gate, watching the crowd dwindle.

At last the players emerged from the locker room, some with their hair still damp from the showers.

Christie's heart raced when Scott came through the gate.

"Hi," he said.

"Hi. You were great!" she said excitedly. Then she noticed a large red welt under his left eye. It would be an ugly bruise by tomorrow. "Are you okay?"

"Yeah. I'm fine." He smiled. His soft voice and relaxed manner betrayed nothing of the fiery football player who had just led his team to victory.

They talked for a few minutes. Christie felt happy in his presence. She felt as she had in grade school when she first started to think of boys as dates instead of pains in the neck. Christie and Scott stood there just looking at each other.

"Hi, beautiful!" Hawk called as he came through the gate. The spell was broken.

"Good game, Scott, old buddy."

"You weren't bad yourself," Scott replied, still gazing at Christie. He seemed to want to say something more to her, but then he turned and walked off.

She stared after him as Hawk took her arm.

"The Eagle's this way," Hawk said. He put his arm around her shoulders as they walked to his jeep.

The parking lot at Quick's Drive-In was full of cars with Trojan bumper stickers. Hawk led Christie through the crowd inside, stopping occasionally to talk to admirers congratulating him on his game. At last they reached a booth where Rod Banners was seated with a guy and another girl.

"Squeeze two more in?" Hawk asked.

"Always room."

Hawk let Christie slide into the seat first, then sat down next to her and made introductions. "This is Christie Moncrieff. Whatever you do, don't call her Goldilocks. She's liable to punch you. This is Al Squires and Ginny Means. You know Rod already. I'll get us a couple of Cokes."

Hawk left, and Christie turned to Rod. "Where's Dee?"

Rod met her eyes squarely, then looked across the room to another booth. There sat Dee, a vacant space beside her, as if she were waiting for someone. Christie wanted to wave to her new friend, but Dee's head was turned away.

"Wouldn't you rather she sat here instead of us?" Christie asked Rod.

"Not particularly," Rod said, stirring his soda absently.

Christie thought she must be seeing the beginning of a lovers' quarrel and decided she'd better not say anything more about it. She'd talk to Dee later to see if she could help. Maybe Dee would like someone to confide in.

Hawk returned with two Cokes and squeezed into the booth beside her, putting his arm around her shoulders.

"Let me give you some killer facts," he told the

29

group. "Killer fact number one: Bethel's got the best defense in the state. Killer fact number two: We've got the best passing attack in the state. Killer fact number three: Our coach, old 'Football Fred' Anderson, is the best in the state. And killer fact number four: We're going to go all the way to the state championship again!"

"That might not be a fact, but I'd say we've got a fair chance at it," Rod said soberly.

"Whatta ya mean, a chance?" Al joined in. He was a big redhead with a bandage above his right eye. "Look at what we just did to Macon City, and the *Register* had them rated tenth in Class 2A."

"The *Register* rates all the schools near Des Moines too high," countered Rod. "There's still some tough competition out there."

"He's a real worrywart. No faith," Hawk said, squeezing Christie's shoulders. "They have worriers like him back in Glen Ellyn?"

She laughed off the question.

As the talk about football continued, Christie looked over at Dee's booth. But Dee had left. She must really be upset with Rod, thought Christie. She wondered what awful thing could have changed things between them so quickly.

The crowd in the restaurant began to thin.

"Ready to go?" Hawk asked, winking.

"Sure," Christie said, looking at her watch. It was almost midnight, and she wanted to get home.

They said good-bye to Rod, Al, and Ginny, and headed for the jeep.

The night air was fresh, and Christie leaned her head against the seat as they drove along. Hawk was keeping his promise to drive carefully. The wind blew her hair back. Heavy clouds moving in from the west crept in front of the moon, and except for the headlights, illuminating a small section of the road before them, Christie and Hawk were enveloped in darkness.

The steady drone of the jeep's engine relaxed Christie. She felt peaceful and content.

Things were going so much better, she thought. The evening had been fun, and she was beginning to feel a sense of belonging in Bethel. What a difference a few days could make. The awful conversation in the locker room had had her feeling as low as she could ever remember. She had felt as unhappy as Dee looked at Quick's. Poor Dee. Christie wanted to be friends and hated to see her so disturbed about Rod.

As they neared her house, Christie's tranquillity gave way to an unexplainable feeling of anxiety. Suddenly, she wanted urgently to get home. She wished Hawk would drive faster. He had driven too fast on the way home from school, but now he was going too slow. Was he trying to annoy her? No. He was only driving the way she had asked him to. What was the matter with her? Her parents hadn't given her a curfew, but she felt she had to get home quickly.

"*Criosdan*."

She thought she heard that voice again, low and rasping. Where had it come from? Did Hawk say something? As Christie glanced at him, she thought she heard it again. This time she was sure

Hawk hadn't said anything. A chill rose along her spine. What was going on?

Christie sat up straight, no longer at ease, and peered out into the darkness. Something out there was calling to her, waiting for her.

"Another mile, and we'll be there."

The sound of Hawk's voice startled her. She shivered and tried to gather her wits.

"You okay, Christie?"

"I'm fine," she said, trying to convince herself that she really was.

"My driving's not bothering you, is it? I'm doing my best to hold it down. When old Hawk slows down for a chick, you know he's serious."

"No. No problem." She tried to sound light-hearted, but the ominous feeling persisted. She couldn't shake the sensation that there was something out there in the darkness, something crouched like a panther waiting for its prey to come within range.

It wasn't like her to have unreasonable fears. I can't let this get to me, she thought. But she shivered in spite of her resolve. Christie stared out into the night. Even the dark of the trees along the road seemed to move menacingly.

At last Hawk turned the jeep into her lane. She almost expected to see someone waiting for them behind the pillars of the porch. But the headlights played on emptiness.

"Home safe and sound once again," Hawk said merrily.

They got out of the car and walked to the door. Christie saw nothing unusual, but she couldn't shake the feeling that a sinister presence was beside her.

Hawk took her arm, turned her toward him, and held her close. "You know, Christie, I could really learn to like you. Awfully easy." He kissed her firmly on the lips.

Christie shuddered slightly. She wasn't ready for this. Christie liked Hawk, but she wasn't sure he was someone she wanted to get seriously involved with. He was a little too sure of himself, a little too pushy. He tried to pull her closer. She drew back, but he was persistent. She wished Hawk would leave.

"*Criosdan*."

Christie thought she heard that harsh whisper again.

"I have to go in." Her voice quavered.

"You feeling all right?" Hawk's voice seemed to come from a great distance.

"No, I'm not. I don't know what's the matter, but all of a sudden I feel a little funny."

"Christie, come on, it was just a friendly kiss."

"I know, Hawk. I just don't feel quite right. I had fun. But I have to go in now."

"Okay. I'll give you a call tomorrow."

"Fine." Christie turned sharply and hurried inside.

Her parents had left the living room light on for her.

She switched it off and headed for the stairs. But suddenly she felt drawn to the barn. She hurried down the dark hallway to the kitchen and out the back door.

The grass was damp with dew and wet her feet as she made her way to the gate of the horse lot. She could see the dim shape of the barn through the blackness of the oak woods.

"*She's coming, my beauty,*" a low demonic voice whispered. Fear gripped her.

As if in a trance, Christie slid the latch, swung the gate open, and closed it behind her. Her fright ebbed, and a marvelous tranquillity filled her. As she entered the woods something familiar seemed to envelope her. It was a delicious sensation of intimacy, as if she was drawing close to someone who knew and understood her.

"*She's coming, coming, coming, coming . . .*" The words swirled around her like phantom birds. She walked through the darkness under the trees. She hadn't thought to bring the flashlight, but it didn't matter. Not a breeze stirred the leaves overhead. The only sound was the rustle of her footsteps in the fallen leaves.

When she reached the barn, she took hold of the door handle. It felt strangely cold as she undid the latch. The door slid open, and as she stepped inside, she was swallowed in blackness. She felt around for the light switch, and quickly turned on the barn lights.

Deep shadows arched across the walls, giving the interior of the barn an eerie appearance. But Christie was not afraid.

Prince was in the center of his stall, gazing into her eyes, waiting for her. He stood calmly, and in the strange light of the barn he appeared somehow larger than usual, his coat ebony and glistening.

Christie thought he had never looked so beautiful before.

She picked up his brush and walked slowly toward him. He bent his great head down to nuzzle her and made a deep, snuffling sound of affection. She felt his warm breath and ran her fingers over the shiny brass ornament dangling from his bridle.

Suddenly, the shadows seemed to close around her, and she felt another presence.

A coarse laugh rose from the shifting shadows up in the rafters. Was there a man looking down at her, a man dressed in animal skins, with something glittering on his chest? Shadows could play strange tricks, she told herself.

Prince's flesh felt warm as she stroked him. Her body quivered, a delicious sensation filling her. She was happier than she had ever been, but she knew that what she felt was unnatural, forbidden. She felt that someone was watching her, and her confusing feelings only partially covered her fear that he was waiting with terrible certainty for her to take another step into the unknown.

Chapter Four

Bright sunlight bathed Christie's face, slowly rousing her from sleep. As her mind rose toward consciousness, she smelled the sweet aroma of hay and felt the hard ground beneath her. Her tired body struggled against awakening, but as her mind cleared, she heard the sound of breathing. Frightened, she opened her eyes to see a horse's hooves. Quickly she sat up. She was in the barn with Prince, who was munching his hay peacefully.

He was the Prince she knew, small and gray. Not at all like the animal she had seen last night. The towering dark animal must have appeared in a dream. Christie looked around, trying to figure out what had happened.

She vaguely remembered walking to the barn after Hawk brought her home from the game. She must have fallen asleep and dreamed of a great stallion. The animal she recalled so vividly couldn't have been Prince. The horse in her dream had been large and black.

Christie remembered that she'd dreamed the night before of a wild ride through a rocky countryside behind an unknown horseman. The ride had ended as before, on a high point of land overlooking the farmhouse and the barn.

Recalling how real her strange dreams had seemed, she shivered. Was she losing her mind? What a foolish thought. Maybe she'd been more exhausted by the excitement of a good day than she'd realized. She must have lain down to rest soon after she got to the barn. But Christie couldn't shake her uneasiness. She remembered the terrible anxiety that she'd felt on the way home. Had that been part of her dream too? She couldn't seem to separate reality from the fabric of her dreams.

She glanced at her wristwatch. It was ten thirty! She never slept this late. What if her parents had gone to her room to look for her? They wouldn't think to look for her in the barn. They would worry if they couldn't find her.

Christie got to her feet quickly, brushing the dirt and straw from her clothes. When she reached the house, she opened the back door as quietly as she could. She could hear her parents talking in the kitchen. Everything seemed normal. The murmur of conversation and the clinking of silver were reassuring. They hadn't realized that she hadn't spent the night in her room. Carefully she crept down the hall to the stairs. No one heard her. She went to her room and changed into her robe and slippers, then went to the bathroom to freshen up.

When she came into the kitchen, her mother looked up cheerfully.

"Good morning, dear. You certainly slept late."

"How was the game?" her father asked.

"It was great. We won easily." Relief flooded through her. They hadn't missed her. Nothing was wrong.

The phone rang a little after one o'clock that afternoon.

"It's for you, Christie," her mother called.

It was Hawk.

"How are you?" he asked. "Feeling okay? You turned pretty weird last night."

"Yes, I'm much better," she replied. "I don't know why I felt the way I did. Maybe I'm getting a cold."

"Do you feel well enough to go to a movie tonight?"

"I'd better not. I'm still a little shaky. I'd better stay in tonight." It was true. She still wasn't over the effects of the evening before.

After they hung up, Christie thought seriously about Hawk. He was nice, and she enjoyed being with him, but she didn't want to be tied down. Not yet, anyway, and probably not to Hawk. She was just beginning to make friends and needed to give herself time to meet other people.

Scott's face flashed into her mind. His quiet self-assurance made her feel warm all over. He was not at all like Hawk. Hawk was a whirlwind, crazy and aggressive. Scott, on the other hand, seemed to have a hidden strength. He boasted less, but he was the one who had taken over on the football field, the undisputed team leader. She remembered his strong, sure hands performing the experiment in biology lab, his quiet face with the lock of black hair brushed across his forehead. I could learn to like him, thought Christie. Yes, I could like him a lot.

She felt like talking to Dee, who knew both Scott and Hawk. Maybe she'd be able to give Christie some advice. Christie didn't want to hurt Hawk, and she wanted to know more about Scott. Perhaps she could help Dee with her problem with Rod, too. After all, that's what girlfriends were for.

Christie spent the afternoon doing chores and working on her algebra assignments. The day was warm and sunny, and she opened the windows of her room wide to let in the sun and the soft autumn breeze. As the hours passed, her memory of the night before began to fade.

But when it was time for Prince's evening feeding, Christie's anxiety returned. She felt reluctant to go to the barn.

This is ridiculous, she told herself. There's a perfectly logical explanation for what happened last night. I was tired, overly excited from meeting so many people. Maybe I was getting sick on top of that. Nothing weird happened. I just fell asleep in the barn—which was dumb, not strange.

Chiding herself for being so foolish, Christie went down to the kitchen, grabbed an apple from the basket on the table, and went out the back door. Prince was grazing peacefully in his pasture and came trotting to her. He made playful passes around her, then stopped to have his ears scratched.

She laughed at his playfulness and held out the apple for him to eat.

She was relieved to see things were normal. The warm sun shone down on the pasture, a squirrel played in a nearby tree, and Prince was just Prince. What had happened last night was simply a dream. It was silly to let herself imagine it could have been real. She laughed out loud and gave Prince a pat on the neck.

When Christie went into the barn everything seemed to be in order. Prince stood quietly outside, waiting at a distance. Christie heard a soft rustling sound in the hay. Suddenly, Prince turned and bolted across the pasture. Christie jumped as she heard what sounded like an evil, mocking laugh. Gasping, she raced out of the barn and headed for the house.

Christie tried to appear calm at the dinner table. She told her parents about the football game and the people she'd met. Her mother suggested she invite someone over for the evening, maybe even to sleep over.

"I might ask Dee. We talked about listening to records together. You'll like her. She's got the neatest blond hair that comes all the way to her waist."

After she helped her mother clear the table, Christie went to the telephone and dialed Dee's number.

"Hello," Dee answered.

"Hi, Dee. This is Christie."

The line was silent for so long that Christie began to think they had been cut off.

"Oh, hi," Dee said at last, her voice lifeless.

"I was wondering if you'd like to come over and listen to some records tonight?"

"I'm busy tonight."

"What about tomorrow? It's Sunday, and any time would be fine with me."

"No. I can't tomorrow either." Dee's voice sounded rather cold, polite, but not friendly. For a moment Christie wondered if she was talking to the right person.

The conversation ended quickly. Dee's lack of responsiveness stopped any attempt Christie made to extend it.

Christie thought about the uncomfortable conversation for a moment, her hand still on the phone. Dee must be terribly upset to have sounded the way she did.

There was nothing good on TV, so she told her parents she was going to her room to read. She carried a soda to her bedroom, turned on the lamp next to her bed, and propped up the pillows so she could sit up. A gentle breeze drifted through the curtains. The words on the page blurred as she became drowsy. Before she knew it, the book had fallen to her lap, and she was asleep.

She awoke with a start. At first she didn't realize what had awakened her, but then the sound of a horse neighing drew her attention to the window. She knocked her book aside and hurried to the window. Out in the darkness she could hear Prince's frantic whinnying and the sound of his hooves kicking the sides of his stall. What was the matter? Why was he doing that? Something must have frightened him. Should she go and see what was wrong?

Her lighted clock said it was fifteen minutes past midnight. Christie had almost decided to go down to the barn, when the noise stopped, and all was quiet again.

I'm being silly, she thought. Probably a skunk or a raccoon got into Prince's stall and scared him. There's certainly nothing out there that can hurt him.

Christie went back to her bed and climbed in. But when she finally fell back asleep, it was to dream once again of a terrifying yet exhilarating ride behind the wild horseman.

Chapter Five

"Christie! Christie Moncrieff!"

It was the drama teacher, Mrs. Burnham, calling to Christie in the hallway on Monday morning. She was a short, thin woman of about fifty who wore too much makeup and a hairdo that made her look as if she'd stuck her finger in a light socket. Mrs. Burnham gestured elaborately and spoke in stagy accents. Apparently she thought this was the way a drama teacher should act. Christie stopped and waited as the teacher fluttered up to her.

"Yes, Mrs. Burnham."

"Christie, dear," she said, her hands waving in the air. "I've been wanting to talk to you. Nell Higgins, who's been in charge of costume design for the school play, has mono and will be out of school for who knows how long. Performances are in eight weeks, and we desperately need a replacement. I asked Mrs. Howard if she could suggest someone to take over the job, and she recommended you. Very highly, I might add. Could you, would you, do it, dear?"

Mrs. Howard was Christie's home economics teacher and had complimented her on the dress she was making in class. Christie thought quickly. Mrs. Burnham was a little flaky, but working on the play would be a chance to meet more people, and it sounded like fun.

"I'd love to try, Mrs. Burnham. What do I have to do?"

"Oh, that's excellent, dear. We meet right after sixth period in the auditorium. You come and meet everyone, and we can talk about the costumes afterward. You'll pretty much have a free hand, and you'll have volunteers to help you with the sewing. By the way, Reginald Jones, from the fine arts department at Iowa State University, is a good friend of mine and will be helping out as a consultant. Mrs. Howard says you're fabulously talented, and if you're interested in pursuing a career in fashion design, Reginald's not a bad person to know." Mrs. Burnham stopped to catch her breath. "Poor Nell. It's a terrible time for her to get sick. She was so looking forward to doing the costumes." The drama teacher turned and said, "Well, see you after sixth period."

"Oh, Mrs. Burnham," Christie called after her.

"Yes, dear?"

"What play are we doing?"

"Oh, my, didn't I say? It's *Man of La Mancha.* The story of Don Quixote, you know. Ever so much fun, don't you think?"

She fluttered off down the hall.

It does sound like fun, thought Christie. And it would give her a chance to meet Reginald Jones. She had heard of him. The clothes he designed were in all the fashion magazines. She and her mother had been to one of his shows in Chicago. It was the best luck. If Nell Higgins hadn't come down with mono, Christie would never have gotten this chance. What a break! Christie was ecstatic.

She had been kidding when she complained to Prince that the only wish he hadn't granted was to make her a fashion designer, she thought superstitiously. Now she was going to design the costumes for the play and would even have a chance to meet Reginald Jones! It was just coincidence, of course. How foolish to think that maybe Prince could make her wishes come true! What harm could it do? He was her friend. She'd give him an extra lump of sugar tonight.

Christie was looking for Dee in the cafeteria when Hawk came up to her.

"Hi, angel. How's my favorite girl?"

"Hi, Hawk. Much better."

"What's for lunch? Hockey puck on a bun and mystery soup?

She laughed. "No. It's tongue of shoe and french-fried laces."

"All right! My favorite!"

"Have you seen Dee?" she asked.

"No, I haven't," Hawk answered, turning his eyes away.

"Are she and Rod having some sort of problem?"

Hawk gave her a questioning look. "Not that I know of."

"They seem to be avoiding each other. When I called Dee Saturday, she seemed pretty upset. I assumed it was because of Rod."

Hawk looked away, shrugging his shoulders as if he didn't care to continue the conversation.

"They have any sole gravy to go with that tongue of shoe?" he asked. The subject had been dropped.

They had their meal tickets punched and found a table. Soon Al Squires and Ginny Means joined them. Then Dee and Rod came through the line. Rod looked their way and nodded. But Dee was intent on choosing her lunch and didn't see them. When they had their meal tickets punched, the pair went to a vacant table at the far end of the cafeteria.

Why didn't Rod tell her we were sitting here? Christie wondered. We have room for them. She had so wanted to talk to Dee. But maybe Dee and Rod needed to be by themselves. That must be it. If they were getting over a fight, they probably needed some time alone to work things out. Hawk was a typical male, thought Christie. He had completely missed the signs of a lovers' quarrel. It took a woman to spot those things.

"How about a ride home in the old Eagle?" he asked as they dumped their trays.

"I've got to stay for a drama club meeting," she said. "Nell Higgins was working on costumes for the school play, but she got mono, and Mrs. Burnham asked me to substitute for her. I have to meet her after rehearsal to find out what has to be done."

"No problem. I've got nothing to do. I'll hang around and watch."

Christie cringed. She wished Hawk wouldn't be so pushy. How could she discourage him without hurting his feelings?

"Thanks, but the meeting may run late. You don't need to wait around. I'll give my parents a call when I'm finished. They can pick me up." If only he would take the hint and cool it a little.

"Okay. I'll call you later. Maybe we can run out for something to eat."

"We'll see. It's a school night, and I don't go out much during the week."

Hawk nodded, shrugging his shoulders, and walked down the hall.

Biology was a bore. Mr. Abernathy lectured on the alimentary canal. The class had to listen to him explain all the gross things that happened to food as it made its way through a person's body. Christie hated to think about the awful things that went on inside her, and her mind wandered.

She sat three rows away from Scott. At least he was in front of her, so she could watch him without being obvious. Mr. Abernathy droned on, and

Christie lost track of what he was saying. Instead of listening, she studied Scott's profile. His handsome face changed often. At times his eyebrows raised, as he seemed to ponder a point Mr. Abernathy was making. Occasionally the muscles in his jaw flexed unconsciously, giving a different line to his clean-cut chin. His full black hair shone in the sunlight, the unruly lock curling willfully across his forehead.

Christie thought she just might be falling in love. Just looking at Scott made her feel shivery and nervous. Christie smiled to herself and realized she was blushing. She looked around quickly to see if anyone noticed her grin. She imagined being alone with Scott on a dark, warm night, and the fantasy filled her with pleasure.

The loud ring of the bell at the end of class startled Christie, bringing her back to reality. She sighed as she saw Scott quickly leave the room before she could gather her books. Out in the hall she looked both ways, but he was gone.

Too bad, thought Christie.

More than twenty kids sat in the first two rows of the auditorium, chattering as Mrs. Burnham called out names and made pencil checks on her clipboard. Sue Ellen, sitting in the row across from Christie, gave her a brief stare and turned away. Three or four other students nodded pleasantly at Christie.

"Okay! Let's come to order!" chirped Mrs. Burnham. "First I want you to meet Christie Moncrieff, who has so kindly consented to take

Nell Higgins' place doing costumes. We all know that Nell is ill, don't we? Poor thing. We wish her well, but the show must go on, as they say. All right, dears. Listen carefully now to your director. Professionalism is the thing."

Mrs. Burnham bounced back and forth in front of the seated students, giving instructions with elaborate gestures.

Christie watched as the teacher took groups onstage and ran them through their parts. Joel Wright, a boy with real acting ability, played Don Quixote. Sue Ellen had the part of Dulcinea, the woman he fell in love with. Christie thought that Sue Ellen overacted, but her singing voice was excellent. There was cheerful banter between the cast and the stage crew. Christie was glad that she had agreed to help.

After a while Christie slipped out of her seat to call home.

"Hello," her mother answered.

"Hi. It's me."

"Hi, dear."

"I've been asked to help out with the school play," Christie explained. "We're meeting right now. Could you pick me up in about half an hour?"

"Of course, dear," her mother said. "What are you doing in the play? Do you have a part?"

"No. I'll tell you all about it when I get home. I've got to meet the director right now."

"Okay. I'll see you in half an hour. Have fun."

Christie hung up and was about to leave the booth when she heard someone talking about her.

"That Christie Moncrieff comes in and immediately starts stealing boyfriends." It was Sue Ellen's voice. "Dee told me Christie even had the nerve to call her Saturday and invite her over to listen to records. Can you imagine? After she started throwing herself all over Hawk."

"Don't you think Hawk might have had something to do with it?" Christie heard another girl ask.

"I doubt it," Sue Ellen answered. "She comes from Glen Ellyn and expects everyone to fall all over her because she's so rich and her mother's an author and her father's a grain broker. We certainly don't need people coming here and looking down at us."

"Oh, Sue Ellen. Do you really think she's so awful?"

"Well, what about her taking Hawk away from Dee?"

Taking Hawk away from Dee? Christie's stomach seemed to turn over. Oh, no. Here she'd thought Dee and Rod were going together. Now she understood. She remembered the empty seat beside Dee at Quick's. Dee must have been waiting for Hawk. That's why she'd been so distant on the phone. It wasn't because Dee was mad at Rod. She was mad at Christie.

"I guess you're right," the girl answered Sue Ellen. "I've got to get home. See you tomorrow."

"See you."

Sue Ellen and the other girl walked down the hall.

Christie leaned against the inside wall of the phone booth, her eyes closed. They thought she had intentionally taken Hawk away from Dee! She hadn't even known they were going out. Dee had been with Rod at school when she met them. And they'd been together at the game, too. How was she to know things were not what they seemed? No wonder Dee had been so cold. Just when Christie thought things were going well, they had to get complicated again.

She stepped out of the phone booth and went back to the auditorium, but her thoughts weren't on the play. She would have to find a way to straighten out this mess.

Chapter Six

Christie's mother moved the van out of the school driveway onto the street.

"Why the glum face, honey?" she asked. "Something wrong with the play? What are you doing?"

"No, Mom, the play's great. Mrs. Burnham asked me to be in charge of costumes. We're doing *Man of La Mancha,* and it seems like a lot of fun. She said that I'll get all the help I need with the sewing. Besides, Reginald Jones is a consultant, and I should get a chance to meet him."

"Reginald Jones? Whose show we saw in Chicago?"

"That's him. Mrs. Burnham knows him."

"Well, that's great. But it certainly doesn't explain your sad face."

"Oh. I just realized I messed up something else pretty badly. You know Dee? I was telling you about her the other day."

"The girl with the blond hair down to her waist?"

"Right. Well, I thought she was going out with a guy named Rod Banners. I saw them together a couple of times. I really thought she and I could be good friends. But actually Dee's going out with Hawk. She's seen me with him a couple of times, and I'm afraid she's mad at me."

"You certainly do have a problem."

"That's not all. I overheard two girls talking about it. They seem to think I'm purposely trying to take Hawk away from Dee."

"And how do you feel about Hawk?"

"He's nice, but I don't want to be attached to him. If I had known they were a couple, I would have turned down the date the other night. He's a little possessive, and I don't want that right now. I've just started to get to know people here."

"Well, I'd suggest that you talk to Dee, tell her your side of the story."

"Yeah, I guess you're right. I'll call her tonight and see if we can straighten things out."

Christie took a plastic milk container with her when she went to the barn. After she fed and watered Prince, she tied the container onto a post in his stall and carefully surveyed the barn. The sound of Prince's frightened neighing the other night had left her feeling uneasy all day Sunday, and she'd been reluctant to spend much time in the barn. But now, telling herself her fears were silly, she tried to figure out what could have upset him. Christie looked around for a hole that a skunk might have crawled through. But the biggest opening she found was only large enough for a mouse to squeeze through.

Christie turned to the horse and patted him on the rump. "Hey, Prince, since when are you afraid of mice? They're always getting in here. You weren't dreaming that you were being ridden in a wild, rocky place, were you? Like in my dream?"

She smiled affectionately at him, but the thought made her shiver. Leaving the barn, Christie looked around outside for any sign that someone had been there. But she saw nothing unusual. There, she thought. That just proves my imagination was working overtime.

As she headed for the house, she noticed the sun was strangely low in the sky. The weather had turned colder since the week before, and winter was in the air. She wondered if Iowa winters were as bad as she had heard. Her dad said that every winter people got trapped on the country roads during blizzards, and if help couldn't reach them, they froze to death. Christie shivered again and headed for the house.

After dinner Christie decided to call Dee.
Dee answered after the second ring. "Hello?"
"Hi. This is Christie."
The line was silent.

"I need to talk to you, Dee. I just found out that you and Hawk are a couple."

"Not now," came Dee's soft response.

"Hey, I'm sorry that I went to Quick's Drive-In with him. If I had known about the two of you, I wouldn't have." She waited anxiously for Dee to say something.

The line was silent a moment longer. At last Christie heard Dee say, "You mean you didn't know?"

"No, I didn't. Really. I saw you with Rod a couple of times and figured you were going out with him."

"Rod?"

"Yes. Rod."

Dee's laugh sounded halfhearted. "Rod's just a buddy," she said.

"Well, I had no way of knowing. I'm sorry, Dee."

"I guess it's not your fault. Hawk's free to do what he wants, and he usually does." Dee sounded depressed.

"Look, I promise you that I won't go out with him again. Okay?" Christie asked.

"I don't know if that will do any good. If Hawk is interested in you, he's not interested in me. If you turn him down, he'll probably just ask someone else." She paused. "I do appreciate your calling, Christie."

"Can we be friends, Dee?"

"Sure. I'm sorry too. I shouldn't have gotten mad. This isn't the first time that Hawk has gone wandering. He's always come back before. I guess he will this time, too."

"You like him a lot, don't you?"

"Yes, maybe more than I should. I never date anyone else. Even when he's not asking me out."

"Let's get together and listen to records sometime, okay?"

"Great," said Dee.

Christie had some trouble keeping away from Hawk during the next few weeks. She didn't want to hurt his feelings, and his constant good humor made it difficult to ignore him. She tried involving herself in the school play. It helped get her mind off him and was lots of fun as well.

School work kept her busy too. Mr. Rathbun, her history teacher, assigned a paper on ancient peoples of the British Isles. The class studied the Romans, the Vikings, and others who had come to Britain in the ancient times.

Christie was especially interested in the Picts, a mysterious race that lived in Scotland one thousand years before the Romans came. According to family legend, the Moncrieffs were descended from them. Her grandfather had written down all the tales he'd heard as a boy about the old country and the clan. When Christie was a little girl, he would get out his old notebook, turn the yellowing pages, and tell her about her ancestors. Like the Picts themselves, who had disappeared so long ago, the Moncrieffs had lived in the highlands of Scotland. Grandfather said the wild, strong people of his branch of the family claimed that the hot, fiery Pict blood ran in their veins.

Christie checked several books out of the library so she could learn more about the ancient clan. She read that the Picts, or *Cruithni,* were pagans who spoke a language believed to be a mixture of Celtic and a lost tongue dating back to the Bronze Age. They were a fierce people, hunters who wore animal skins and tattooed their faces and bodies. They had warlike ways, performed secret rituals and survived the rugged mountains where they lived. Christie liked the strange-sounding names of their towns and lakes including Dunkeld, Atholl, Oweynagat, Shiehallion, and Tobar Caoch.

Their art was interesting too, and in some way it seemed oddly familiar to Christie. Stylized drawings of a large animal called the Pictish Beast appeared in all the books. Christie found the creature both repulsive and fascinating. With a sense of shock she finally realized why it looked so familiar. The animal on the old horse brass, the ornament on Prince's bridle, was one and the same!

The next day at lunch Christie's mind was still on the Picts. She hoped she'd find something to make her assignment more interesting in the trunk where her grandfather had kept his papers. She'd go through it after school.

Christie sat with Dee, while Hawk ate with other kids. Now and then she saw him looking in their direction, but he didn't come over. Sitting with Dee was one way to get Hawk to keep his distance, she realized. She and Dee talked nervously at first. Gradually, though, they overcame their awkwardness, and they chatted as if nothing had happened. Christie hoped that she and Dee could become best friends. It would be good to have someone her own age to confide in.

After lunch Christie went to Mrs. Burnham's room. In addition to reading up on the Picts, she had researched the Spain of Don Quixote and had made preliminary sketches for the costumes she had in mind.

Mrs. Burnham pored over the drawings, muttering, "Oh, my! Oh, yes!"

Finally she looked up and said, "Excellent, my dear. And just in time, too."

"Just in time, Mrs. Burnham? I didn't think you needed them until next week."

"Actually I don't, but Reginald is coming tomorrow, and I would so like to show these to him."

"Reginald Jones, Mrs. Burnham?" Christie's eyes opened wide.

"Who else, dear? We did know that he was assisting us with the play, didn't we?"

"Yes, we, er, I did, but I didn't know that he was coming tomorrow."

"Well, he is, my dear. And I will show these exquisite drawings to him. I'm sure he'll be simply thrilled."

Christie left Mrs. Burnham's room in fine spirits. Reginald Jones was going to look at her sketches! Would he like them? Should she go home and work on them some more? Calm down, she told herself. These drawings are pretty good, but no one expects a finished product yet. She decided not to alter them before Mr. Jones had a chance to advise her. It wouldn't be professional. She laughed at herself. She was beginning to sound like Mrs. Burnham. The next thing she knew, she'd be waving her hands extravagantly as she spoke.

Chapter Seven

When she got home from school that afternoon, Christie felt on top of the world. Tomorrow Reginald Jones was going to look at her drawings. It was the chance of a lifetime.

She studied the sketches of Dulcinea's costume. She liked it. Maybe she was being immodest, but she was truly proud of the design. She wasn't sure that she liked the idea of Sue Ellen wearing the dress, though. Why did Sue Ellen have it in for her? Was she still angry because she thought Christie had tried to steal Hawk from Dee? Sue Ellen didn't seem to be that close to Dee, so why did she care? Christie couldn't help but remember that Sue Ellen had acted hostile toward her even before she had met Hawk. Hawk couldn't be the problem.

There are better things to think about than Sue Ellen. She was beginning to feel that Bethel was a nice place to live. It's not Glen Ellyn, Christie told herself, but there are some nice people like Dee and Scott. Hawk, too. He just needed to understand that she wasn't interested in going out with him. Rod and Lisa and the others were fun too. Before long she might be really happy in Bethel. Especially if things worked out between her and Scott. She felt warm inside at the thought of him.

The sound of the ringing telephone broke into her thoughts.

"Hello," she answered.

"Hi, it's Dee. Is that offer to come over and listen to records still on?"

"You bet it is!"

"Are you free now?"

"Sure. I'm not doing much."

"How do I get to your house?"

"Just go north of town. Our lane is right across from Izaak Walton Park."

"Good. I'll be there in about ten minutes."

Dee arrived with an armload of records.

"You've got some I don't have," Christie said, sorting through the stack. "This one I really like."

She put the record on the turntable and set the volume so they could listen and talk at the same time.

"I'm glad you called the other day," said Dee. "I was feeling pretty low and confused, and I guess I blamed you more than I should have."

"No problem," responded Christie. "Let's forget it."

"How's the play coming? Gee, those are great

drawings," she commented, noticing the sketches.

"I'm really excited. Tomorrow Mrs. Burnham's showing my drawings to Reginald Jones from Iowa State."

"Is that good?"

"Only the greatest. He's nationally known, and I can't wait to hear what he has to say about my designs. I just hope——"

She was cut off by the ringing of the phone.

"Hello."

"Hi. What are you doing?" It was Hawk. Christie's heart sank. She hoped Dee wouldn't realize who it was, but she felt awkward.

"I'm listening to records with Dee," she said softly.

"Oh." He hesitated. "I won't keep you then, but how about going out after the game Friday?"

"No, I don't think so."

"How come? Someone else moving into my territory?"

"No. I'd just rather not."

"Say, look. I know that you know that Dee and I have been seeing each other, but we're not married. If I want to date someone else, why shouldn't I? If she wanted to do the same, it would be her right. How would you feel about it if she did? Would she wear the black hat then?"

He was entangling Christie in a conversation that wasn't going to be easy to get out of. She glanced at Dee, who was studying a record cover.

"I'd rather not talk about it right now."

Dee looked up quickly, a look of painful comprehension on her face.

"I've got to go," Christie said in a rush. She

didn't want to hurt him, but there was no other way out.

"Okay, if that's the way you want it," said Hawk. He sounded angry for the first time since she had known him.

He hung up before she could say anything more.

Christie slowly replaced the phone in its cradle and turned to Dee, whose eyes were beginning to fill with tears.

"It was Hawk, wasn't it?" Dee asked quietly.

"Yes." There was nothing more Christie could say.

They listened to records for a little while, but Dee was obviously depressed. Finally she made an excuse to go.

Christie felt terrible. She put away her records and decided to feed Prince before supper.

A heavy chill hung in the late October air, as she made her way down to the barn just before sunset. She hurried. Christie had avoided going to the barn after dark ever since she had fallen asleep there that night, even though she'd convinced herself it was foolish to be afraid. Prince stood quietly as she poured his grain and did not move to eat as she checked his water.

"Oh, Prince, everything's such a mess! I hope things are simpler for you." He moved close to her, as if trying to understand. She scratched him behind the ears and touched his brass ornament, studying the odd picture of the Pictish Beast.

"I wish Hawk would just go away. It would make things a lot easier." With a start she recalled that the other times she'd confided in Prince her wishes had come true. Would this one come true? She shivered. What a thought. The other times had just been coincidences. She laughed at herself, but her laugh echoed hollowly.

Prince nuzzled her as if he sympathized.

Christie patted him, and he moved closer to her, enjoying the attention. Somehow, when she was was with him, her problems didn't seem as important as they had before.

"Christie!" It was her father calling.

She came out of the barn and saw him at the back gate.

He saw her and yelled, "Dinner!"

She felt unreasonably angry toward her father. But by the time she reached him at the gate, the feeling had dissipated.

He greeted her. "We're having microwave casserole. Your mother's got to meet that book deadline."

"What kind?" she asked.

"Taco."

"Good. That's one casserole I like."

The next morning Christie awoke remembering that she'd had strange dreams all night. She was exhausted and puzzled. She had never dreamed as much as she had in the last two months, and she kept waking up with the ominous certainty that something terrible was about to happen.

In one dream she was at her bedroom window, looking down at the practice lot. There was a horse near the gate, but it wasn't Prince. Again, the animal in her dream was larger and blacker. It stood motionless, gazing up at her window. In the shadows of the woods beyond, she thought she saw the figure of a man. He too seemed to be watching her, waiting. Something shiny glistened on his chest. She heard his low, whispering voice. He seemed to be addressing someone else. *"In time, my beauty. In time."* The words made her blood run cold, and she shivered, yet she was conscious of a yearning she didn't understand.

In another dream she was riding behind the mysterious horseman again. Why were they haunting her?

She shook her head sharply and tried to get the terrible sound of the voice out of her mind. She remembered that this was the day Reginald Jones was going to be at school. Today he would see her drawings.

She dressed quickly, gulped her morning juice and milk, and was out at the end of the lane fifteen minutes early. She was excited about the day ahead of her, yet she couldn't shake the dread that had come over her. These terrible dreams were leaving her drained.

When the bus pulled up, she got on quickly, nodded to the driver, and went to her usual seat at the back.

She was especially impatient this morning and hated all the stops they had to make. It seemed as if every one of the elementary school kids was taking all the time in the world getting on the bus.

They were nearing town, when the bus slowed and came to a stop. Christie saw the flashing red lights of emergency vehicles casting an eerie strobelike effect on the scene. At a signal from a man standing in the road, their driver put the bus into gear and drove slowly forward. As they pulled up to the roadblock, the elementary kids chattered excitedly, and the older kids peered out the windows. But Christie, drenched in sweat, did not want to look.

The bus moved nearer, and the state patrolmen directed traffic away from a ditch where a wrecker crew was pulling out a mangled car. Christie couldn't help but look as one of the men with the wrecker waved his hand, and the car was lifted onto the road.

She froze. It was the Screaming Eagle!

Its crushed hood dangled by one hinge. The roll bars, which were meant to protect its occupants, were twisted and mashed against the seats. The fenders were crumpled, and the tires were flat, except for one that had been torn from its rim. The paint, which usually glistened with wax, was smeared with mud.

Christie was startled by the wail of a siren, as an ambulance moved away from the other emergency vehicles and sped past the bus, its lights flashing.

The words she had spoken in the barn sounded in her head—I wish Hawk would just go away—and she screamed.

Chapter Eight

Tears poured down Christie's cheeks, as the bus headed into town. She buried her face in her hands, and her shoulders shook with deep sobs. Except for Christie's sobbing the bus was silent. The younger kids shot furtive glances at her and then looked away. The driver, shaken by Christie's scream, glanced nervously at the poor girl's reflection in the rearview mirror.

Christie was terrified that Hawk was dead. The wail of the ambulance's siren echoed in her ears. Maybe he'd been thrown free from the Eagle and had landed in the soft field, she told herself. But Christie continued to sob, unable to forget her terrible wish that he would go away. What she'd confided to Prince had come true. Until she'd seen the pathetic wreckage of what had once been Hawk's most prized possession, she'd convinced herself that her innocent desires had become reality through lucky coincidence. But now she was seized by a wrenching guilt.

As the bus stopped in front of Herbert Hoover High, Christie attempted to wipe her tear-stained face, but she couldn't stop crying. She ran to the girls' room as soon as she entered the building. A sorry face looked back at at her from the mirror. Her eyes were puffy, and her makeup had run. She stared at herself. Had she caused Hawk's accident by wishing him gone? She'd wanted him gone, not dead.

Her wishes came true each time she shared them with Prince. What if it wasn't coincidence? Nell Higgins got mono, after Christie told Prince that she wanted to be a fashion designer. Designing costumes for the school play was great experience, and the opportunity to meet Reginald Jones might help her start a career. But did her own good fortune come at another's expense?

She splashed some cool water on her face and tried to calm down. The way Hawk drove, he could have had an accident anytime. It was sad, but not that surprising. The thought made her feel better. She dried her face with a paper towel, gathered her books and drawings, and went to her first class.

Everyone in the school knew about the accident, but no one knew how Hawk was. The school was stunned to hear that Hawk Sloan had been hurt. They were too used to seeing him stride through the school hallways or on the football field, talking and joking with people.

Christie tried to keep her mind on her class work. There was nothing more to do until they found out how Hawk was. She showed Mrs. Howard her drawings and accepted her praise halfheartedly. Christie's mind was on Hawk. She would have to look for Dee between classes. Maybe Dee had heard something about his condition. I hope she already knows about the accident, she thought. I don't want to be the one to tell her the awful news.

The class bell rang. Christie collected her things and went out the door. Rod was there, waiting for her.

"Rod, have you heard anything about the accident? I saw the Eagle being pulled out of a ditch on the way to school. Was Hawk hurt?"

Rod drew in his breath, as if considering what to say. "Hawk wasn't hurt, Christie." He hesitated. "He was killed. Instantly, I'm afraid."

Christie gasped. She was too overcome even to cry. The worst was true. Hawk was dead. She felt faint and swayed slightly.

Rod grabbed her arm. "Are you all right?"

She tried to regain her composure. "Does Dee know?" she asked.

"She knows," Rod said. "She broke down, and Lisa and Al took her home."

Christie leaned against the wall. "Oh, Rod," she sobbed.

He reached out clumsily, put his arms around

her, and held her close, trying to comfort her. He was silent. What was there to say?

Somehow Christie plodded through the rest of the day. Her mind refused to focus on anything her teachers said. She went through her classes mechanically.

Biology was the last class of the day. She sketched in her notebook as the teacher lectured. At one point in the class she saw Scott staring at her.

When the bell rang, he came over to her and put a hand on her arm.

"It's really awful about Hawk," he said. "You all right?"

His eyes were soft and caring.

"I'll be all right. Poor Dee, though. Rod said she had to be taken home."

"I heard," he said. He looked deep into her eyes, as if searching for something and then, apparently satisfied, smiled his sideways grin at her. "You take care," he said quietly.

"I will."

He turned and walked away. She watched him go, following the graceful movement of his athletic body.

Despite Christie's growing sense of alarm, the meeting with Reginald Jones went well. Mrs. Burnham showed him Christie's drawings, and they both held their breath as he looked at them, first placing them side by side on the floor of the stage, then holding each one at arm's length for careful consideration.

"Excellent," he said at last. "These show a lot of talent. You must have done a lot of research on the play."

"I tried," Christie said.

Mrs. Burnham beamed.

"I have a couple of minor suggestions you might want to consider. One has to do with Sancho Panza's costume, and the other with Dulcinea's dress. But other than that, I think you've done an excellent job. I'd like to see these when you're ready to begin making them. I might have some suggestions as to sewing techniques."

Mrs. Burnham clasped her hands under her chin. "Didn't I tell you she had talent, Reginald?"

Mr. Jones looked at Mrs. Burnham and smiled. "Yes, Frances, and you were right. There's always room for young people who are talented and willing to work." Turning to Christie, he said, "Young lady, I'm going to have to keep an eye on you."

Christie was thrilled by his words, momentarily pushing her concern over Hawk's tragic death to the back of her mind. Reginald Jones liked her drawings! She could hardly wait to tell her mother and father. It seemed possible that her dream of being a fashion designer might actually come true someday.

Christie's exuberance faded on her way home. She told her parents about the meeting with

Reginald Jones and repeated his encouraging words. Her parents were happy and Christie tried to match their excitement. But then tears filled her eyes, and she sobbed as she revealed the details of Hawk's gruesome death.

When she fed Prince before supper she looked at him closely. He was the same old Prince. There was nothing unusual about him. Why couldn't she shake the thought that he had something to do with her wishes? She was acting like a child. There were no such things as magic lamps and genies that made wishes come true. It was all impossible. She just felt guilty because she had wished things to happen and by coincidence they had. But not in the way she had wanted. She had not wished that Hawk would die.

After supper she tried to do her homework. Her mind kept drifting to Hawk and she couldn't concentrate. Perhaps if she could find her grandfather's notebooks it might help her get involved in her history paper for Mr. Rathbun.

The door to the attic was at the end of the upstairs hallway. She climbed the narrow stairway in the dark. She waved her hand around in circles, searching for the pull string to the only light in the attic. Finally it brushed against her hand. She yanked it, and the room glowed dimly, lit by a single bare bulb.

She hadn't been in the attic since the week they moved in, but she thought she remembered where her grandfather's trunk was. She pushed away the piles of empty moving boxes and searched through the old furniture, which had served generations of Moncrieffs. Her father had shown her the cradle that had been in the family for at least a hundred years and in which all the Moncrieff babies, including himself, had spent their first few months.

Christie found the trunk, undid the latches, and lifted the lid. It opened stiffly, the hinges squeaking in protest.

On top was an assortment of her grandfather's clothes, including his World War I uniform and his Scottish tweed jacket. Under them she found his shaving mug, brush, and razor strop. At the bottom of the trunk were a large Bible and a box that was tied with string.

She pulled the box out of the trunk and loosened the string. When she removed the lid, she found papers and an old notebook.

She smiled and sat back on her heels to read. The pages were yellow with age, and she turned them carefully, trying not to damage them.

The notes were written in her grandfather's careful handwriting.

As she turned the pages, she skimmed the words that told about the ancient Moncrieff clan. The most recent years were described first, so that the story unfolded backward. She saw her father's name on the first few pages. Her grandfather must have stopped writing shortly after her father had left home for college. Christie thought she'd like to continue the Moncrieff story where her grandfather had left off.

At first she turned the pages quickly, eager to reach the part that told about the Moncrieffs who had lived in Scotland. Then, as she began to find what she was looking for, she read more slowly, turning back the years with each flip of a page. The descriptions painted a people whose names and ways were alien. Kneeling in the dimly lit attic, she felt as if she were in a time machine, journeying backward. The stories depicted the ancient Moncrieffs as the wild people her grandfather had spoken about. The pagan Pict blood must have pounded, hot and strong, through their veins.

When Christie came upon the name Cormac Moncrieff she was transfixed. The name filled her with foreboding. She didn't want to read any more, didn't want to know what her grandfather's words would tell her. She closed the book and started to put it back in its box. For a moment she held the book in the air at arm's length. Then she drew it back to her lap. Unable to help herself, she opened the notebook—precisely to the page where she'd seen the disturbing name. Christie shivered at the odd coincidence and found herself irresistibly drawn into the story of her ancestors.

At first Cor Moncrieff had seemed no different from other boys who lived in Scotland two hundred years ago. Then, in his teens, he fell in love with his cousin, Criosdan Moncrieff. He adored the young woman, who was as rough and wild as he was. He swore to give her anything she wished for that could be found on earth. She loved him in return and promised to marry him. Together they rode over the hills and through the glens. But one day she turned against him—no one ever knew why—and took back her pledge to wed him. Cor was furious and refused to accept her decision. He cried out that a promise was sacred: Her pledge to marry him was binding, as were his promises to her. The jealous Cor pursued her, fighting with any young man who looked at her. Then Criosdan caught a fever, and on her deathbed she asked that Cor be brought to her. "If you grant my last wish, I will come with you," she said. But before she was able to reveal her final wish, she fell back upon her pillow, and her eyes closed forever.

Cor Moncrieff seemed to go mad. He would not accept Criosdan's death. He visited an aged hag shunned as an evil witch and became her pupil. She was said to know the old ways of the Picts and taught Cor their secret rituals. Cor tattooed the ancient Pictish Beast on his chest and wore a massive silver chain around his neck, as his ancestors were said to have done.

Cor grew to be a great, dark man with black hair and fiery eyes. Close to the secrets of his pagan roots, he was rumored to be able to do powerful things—he could look at cattle and horses and make them sick, or he could make sick animals well. His eyes seemed to have a hypnotic influence—especially over women. It was said that no woman who looked into Cor Moncrieff's eyes ever wanted another man again.

Cor Moncrieff rode a huge black stallion called Athame, the name given to the black-handled knives witches used in their ceremonies. People said that Athame had mysterious powers. The beast would tilt its head down to listen when Cor Moncrieff whispered in his ear and the aftermath was often a granted wish—good or evil. The favorite horse of a neighbor who angered Cor Moncrieff would suddenly fall ill and die of an unknown disease. Or a woman the neighbor fancied would suddenly fall madly in love with Cor Moncrieff.

Christie wanted to put the book down, but her hands felt glued to it. She was driven to read on.

When people saw Cor Moncrieff ride by their homes at night on the great black Athame, they would lock their doors and close their shutters. Often they heard the thundering hooves of Athame, carrying his master home just before the first light of dawn. There were rumors of young girls who disappeared mysteriously, and some of the neighbors claimed to have heard the girls' high-pitched cries when Cor Moncrieff returned home from his nightly rides. It seemed that since Cor could not have Criosdan, he would punish the world.

The story seemed too fantastic to believe. Like an ancient fable filled with dragons, potions, and evil spells, it just couldn't be true. And yet she trembled as she pictured Cor Moncrieff, dressed in animal skins, a gleaming silver chain around his neck. The faceless rider in her dreams had worn animal skins too. And the night she'd fallen asleep in the barn, she'd thought she'd seen a huge man with something gleaming on his chest. Even Prince had appeared immense and black, exactly as her grandfather's words described Athame.

Had her grandfather ever told her this story? Perhaps during one of her summer visits to the farm, he had mentioned the strange ancestor, and the long-buried memory had made its way into her dreams. But she had always listened attentively to her grandfather's tales and couldn't recall ever hearing about Cor Moncrieff before.

As she recalled the wishes she'd whispered to Prince, the wishes that so oddly had come true, she shuddered. Athame had made Cor Moncrieff's wishes come true as well. The similarity chilled her. Her mind raced. Could she somehow be linked with Criosdan, who died so long ago? She shook her head. The thought was absurd. But still a terrible fear gripped her.

She was drawn back to the notebook. A hunter of the Lindsay clan, who lived in a nearby glen, was bringing home a deer carcass slung across his horse's back when he heard a distant thunder of hooves. He saw a great black horse carrying two figures over the ridge to the west. The figures silhouetted against the red rays of the setting sun he recognized as Cor Moncrieff and a woman.

A terrible suspicion stirred in the hunter's mind. Recently he had seen Cor casting lustful glances at his young wife, and he feared that she had returned those glances.

Rushing into his cottage, the hunter saw their evening meal cooking on the hearth—but his wife was gone. Brokenhearted, he vowed revenge.

In ancient times a burning cross was the signal for a clan rising. Quickly he chopped two tree limbs and bound them together into a cross. He buckled on his double-edged broadsword and set the cross afire, leaping astride his horse to pursue the fleeing couple.

Holding the fiery cross high so that it could be seen by his fellow clansmen throughout the glen, the Lindsay huntsman galloped toward the ridge. As he descended the slope beyond, he rode almost straight into an ambush! Cor Moncrieff had seen him coming and was lying in wait.

As the huntsman stormed down the hillside, brandishing the fiery cross, he saw fear cross Cor's face. He sensed that Cor felt no dread of Clan Lindsay's vengeance. It was the blazing symbol of the cross that struck fear into Moncrieff's pagan heart!

Wedging the torch upright among some rocks, the outraged husband drew his sword. Cor's sword flashed too, as he drew it from its scabbard. The two rushed fiercely at one another, slashing away like madmen, while the hunter's wife cowered anxiously nearby.

The clanging of their blades echoed through the glens. They were fighting on horseback, which gave the huge black stallion's rider advantage. Slowly but surely Cor beat down his enemy. Both were panting and bleeding from their wounds, but at last the Lindsay huntsman toppled from the saddle and landed at his wife's feet.

The guilt-stricken woman trembled. Cor wheeled his mount again. The Lindsay hunter struggled to his feet. He had already seen the black-hearted warlock shrink in fear from the burning cross. Now he dabbled his fingers in his own blood and smeared the X-shaped cross of Scotland on his wife's forehead.

As he did so, he noticed a painted comb in her hair—one he had never seen her wear before. Carved into the wood was the outline of the Pictish Beast. The sight of it made him gnash his teeth in rage. He had heard that Cor gave trinkets to girls who caught his eye, to aid him in winning their love. Here was the gift that had led to his own wife's seduction!

Quivering with hatred, the hunter tore the comb from her tresses and broke it in two. Then he snatched up the burning cross and set the pieces of the ornament on fire. Athame whinnied loudly. He bucked and reared in agony, almost flinging Cor from the saddle.

It was then that the hunter realized that the steed Athame was a demon incarnate. By breaking and burning the image of the Pictish Beast, he had inflicted unbearable punishment on its earthly counterpart! The stallion twisted and plunged wildly, drumming his hooves like thunder. Cor clutched the stallion's mane, trying desperately to keep from being thrown from his seat. The hunter's swift actions seemed to have freed his wife from Cor Moncrieff's power. She retrieved her husband's sword from the ground and handed it back to him. With a fresh surge of strength he attacked Cor furiously and thrust the sword into the wild man's heart.

Trumpeting madly, the black stallion bore his wounded master off into the darkness, never to be seen again. Some said they saw a dark steed that looked like Athame flying with his rider at night, but there was never any evidence that Cor survived.

Christie's hands shook violently as she put down the notebook. If she believed these old stories, she would believe anything. They couldn't have anything to do with her. There was nothing to tie her sudden new friendships, Nell's illness, or Hawk's death to this demon from the past. Her imagination was simply running away with her. An unwelcome thought struck her. The hunter was a Lindsay. And that was Sue Ellen's name too.

"No!" she cried. Angrily, she slammed the notebook closed. She started to put it back in its box, to replace it at the bottom of the trunk. But it slipped from her fingers and fell open again on the floor. A sentence in her grandfather's handwriting stood out on a not-too-yellowed page. "My granddaughter is to be named Christine," it read. "In Gaelic, the tongue of Scotland, that is Criosdan."

Christine leaned against the trunk for a moment, trying to regain her composure. The attic walls seemed to be closing in, the stairway seemed far away, at the end of a long tunnel walled in by the boxes and old furniture. The light over the stairway hung at a strangely precarious angle from the raftered ceiling.

She had to get out of the attic and back to her mother and father, in the house below. Back to reality, where she would be safe. Away from that wretched notebook.

"*She knows, my mighty beast. She knows we're here.*" The words rang through the attic, loud, yet whispered. It was the low, rasping voice she had heard before. She clapped her hands over her ears, but demonic laughter seemed to pound like rain inside her skull. Or was it Criosdan's skull?

Christie shuddered and ran to the narrow stairway, terror still echoing around her. She tripped but regained her balance and threw the door open to escape.

Chapter Nine

Hawk's face was unreal. His skin was changed by the makeup they had put on it. His mouth curved in an artificial smile. Christie thought that if she touched him, he would feel like a department store dummy. There would be no warmth, no resiliency to the skin. She had never before seen him dressed in a suit and tie, as he was now, lying in his casket with his head on a white satin pillow. The clothes added to the feeling of unreality that overwhelmed Christie.

Her eyes brimmed with tears as she bid him good-bye and moved away from the casket. Her mother and father stood beside the casket for a moment, then followed her.

Mr. and Mrs. Sloan sat in the first row. Hawk's father had his arm around his wife, whose grief covered her face.

Dee was seated behind them, her eyes red and her face swollen from crying. Christie's heart went out to her. She wanted to talk to her friend, to comfort her. But how could she? What if Christie herself had been the cause of Hawk's death? She didn't know what to think anymore. What she had read in the notebook made her doubt her own sanity. The strange voice she kept hearing, the dreams that disturbed her sleep made her half believe that Cor Moncrieff had come from the past to fulfill her wishes. Was she somehow linked to the lost Criosdan? How could that be? Yet when she'd read his name, she'd felt she knew Cor Moncrieff. What scared her most was the knowledge that she wanted to see him again.

Sue Ellen sat in the fifth row and frowned as Christie walked by. Sue Ellen Lindsay. It was too much. A net seemed to be tightening around Christie.

The rest of the benches were filled with solemn-faced relatives and friends, waiting respectfully in silence for the service to begin.

Christie found space for herself and her parents two rows in front of Scott. He smiled at her as she made her way past him, but she was almost afraid to smile back.

The organist came into the room through a side door and played a mournful hymn that surged through the room.

The music trailed off as the minister took his place at the front of the church. His words about Hawk might have been said about any young man Hawk's age. He didn't mention Hawk's infectious humor or his constant laughter. That was the Hawk that she knew. Not the boy the minister referred to as Hal Sloan. The minister's words about Hawk were as artificial as the thing that lay in the casket.

At the end of the service the congregation remained seated while the funeral director closed the casket. Hawk's mother moaned when her son's face disappeared beneath the coffin lid. Dee's back shook with silent sobs.

The pallbearers positioned themselves on both sides of the casket as the funeral director placed flower wreaths on top. Then they raised the casket from its stand and carried Hawk up the aisle and through the double doors to the hearse waiting outside.

The long caravan of cars moved slowly toward the cemetery, their headlights illuminated in silent respect. They snaked down the narrow road that wound among the tombstones before stopping near a freshly turned mound of dirt beside the deep hole where Hawk would be laid to rest.

The wind blew across the open fields, as the crowd huddled around the pit in the ground. Dark clouds came out of the west and skimmed low over the top of the brown-leafed oak that kept a lone watch over the graveyard.

Christie held her coat collar closed against the cold.

The ceremony was brief, but she could no longer hold back her tears. Mr. Moncrieff put his arm around his sobbing daughter.

It was during the minister's final words that she noticed Sue Ellen staring at her from the opposite side of the grave. The look she gave Christie was burning with hatred. The story of the Lindsay hunter returned to Christie's mind. What did it have to do with Sue Ellen? Christie shook her head. Nothing seemed to make sense anymore.

The minister finished the service and turned away from the grave.

"I want to say something to Dee before we leave," Christie told her mother and father.

"All right, dear," her mother said. "We'll wait for you at the car."

"Take your time," said her father.

Several people stood talking with the Sloans, and Dee was among them. She saw Christie coming.

"Hi," said Dee. She smiled weakly at Christie.

"Hi. How are you?"

"I'll make it, I guess. It's going to take some getting used to, but I guess I'll be okay." Her eyes moistened as she spoke.

Christie reached out to touch Dee's arm in sympathy.

"You've got a lot of nerve, Christie Moncrieff!"

Startled, Christie turned to Sue Ellen, who had blurted out the words.

The people talking to the Sloans stopped and turned in surprise.

Christie started to speak, but Sue Ellen interrupted, "You threw yourself at Hawk and then tried to make up to Dee! If you had left him alone, he might still be alive today!"

The words stung like stones. Christie had been tortured by guilty fears that she had been the cause of Hawk's death. To hear someone say it out loud was like being punched. She opened her mouth but she did not know what to say. What if Sue Ellen was right? Perhaps in some unearthly, inexplicable way Sue Ellen had stumbled on the terrible truth.

"Why did you have to come to Bethel anyway?" Sue Ellen moved toward her, and Christie stepped back as if she expected a blow.

"Just a minute, Sue Ellen! Christie had nothing to do with Hawk's death." Dee came to Christie's defense.

Scott walked up behind Christie. "Sue Ellen, you'd better think about what you're saying and who you're saying it in front of," he said, looking pointedly at Hawk's parents.

Sue Ellen glared as if she were going to continue her tirade against Christie but then turned angrily and stalked away.

Mr. Sloan took his wife's arm and led her to a waiting car.

"I'm sorry," said Dee. "That was a mean thing for her to say."

Christie tried to smile, but it came off weakly. Sue Ellen had really gotten to her. Her words had brought Christie's private fears out in the open. Could Sue Ellen have known? Could she too be in touch with . . ? No, it was beyond belief.

Scott looked at Christie with a worried frown.

"Come on, Christie. Do you have a ride home?" he asked.

"My mom and dad are waiting for me."

Taking her arm, he walked her to the van, where her parents were waiting.

"We still have to play on Friday. Are you

91

coming to the game?" he asked.

Christie looked up at him. She had not gone to a game since the time with Hawk. She knew the team was winning, and it looked as if they would be in the state play-offs. But now she wondered sadly how the loss of Hawk would affect the team's chances.

"I don't know," she said.

"I'd like to see you after the game," Scott said. "We wouldn't have to go the Quick's. Maybe we could go for a pizza. It would give us a chance to talk."

"I'd like that." She needed someone understanding to talk to. Being alone with Scott might help her sort things out. Maybe she'd finally get a grip on herself. She felt like she was falling apart—and she desperately hoped she could pull herself together. Maybe Scott was the answer.

"Would you mind picking me up after the game?" she asked. The question sounded so normal, Christie thought. She resolved to put on a good show. "I'd love to watch you play, but I don't feel like being in a crowd. Not right now."

"Sure. No problem. I'll pick you up around ten thirty."

He smiled down at her and held her hands for a moment before turning to leave. His soft blue eyes were understanding, and his strong hands transferred some of his assurance. Maybe everything would be okay after all.

Scott called that evening. It was a pleasant, uncomplicated conversation. They talked about the play and Christie's costume designs, about the team and its chances without Hawk. Scott thought they would be hurt but still hoped to get into the play-offs. When they hung up, she felt less anxious. She had really let the Cor Moncrieff thing get out of hand. How could she possibly believe there was any tie between herself and a man, a horse, and a girl who lived generations ago? It was crazy. She had to finish the costume designs for the play, to work on her school work, to try to help Dee, and to get to know Scott better. She especially wanted to get to know Scott better. Christie thought about him. She liked the sound of his name. She smiled to herself looking forward to their date the next evening.

She got ready for bed early, brushing her hair before putting on her nightgown. She opened the window slightly to let in the cool breeze and looked down at the dark, empty horse lot below. Prince was in the barn, and everything was quiet. Silly, she thought. Why I ever let my imagination get out of hand I'll never know. That's not like Christie Moncrieff.

She climbed into bed, turned out the night table light and pulled the covers up under her chin.

She hoped she might dream of Scott. But her night's sleep was troubled and restless.

Chapter Ten

Giovanni's Pizzeria was nearly empty when Scott and Christie arrived. Scott picked up their order at the counter, while Christie sat in a candle-lit booth, waiting for him. He had picked her up with the good news that Bethel had won again, assuring them a place in the play-offs. He was happy, and his excitement pushed her thoughts about Hawk's death and Cor Moncrieff's ancient power to the back of her mind. He was in high spirits. She was glad for him. He had played hard, and the marks of the game showed on his face and hands. Christie felt protective, knowing his body must be covered with bruises.

Scott paid the cashier and came back to the

booth, smiling and holding the pizza above his shoulder like a waiter.

"How does that look?" he asked, setting it down along with two small paper plates and two forks.

"Great! You really know how to wine and dine a girl."

"Soda and dine a girl, you mean!"

They chatted happily while they ate. Being with Scott was relaxing. Even the moments when they had nothing to say weren't strained. They didn't have to fill every moment with talk. Scott was at ease, not always needing to be the life of the party, the way Hawk had. Christie cringed, realizing she was comparing Scott to the dead boy. But Scott was so different from Hawk. Scott seemed content with himself. He was not like anyone she had met before, including Robbie Cranston. Surprised, Christie realized that she hadn't thought about Glen Ellyn in weeks and that it had been even longer since she'd thought of Robbie. She had become so involved in what was happening in Bethel that Glen Ellyn seemed worlds away.

Christie polished off three pieces of pizza and put her fork down. She'd had all that she could eat and sat back to watch Scott devour the rest.

"What are you smiling at?" he asked, looking up at her after the last bite.

"You. You do like to eat."

"I worked up quite an appetite tonight."

"I can understand."

Time slipped by as they talked. Scott told her about his childhood sweetheart. They'd known

96

each other for ten years, but then she'd moved away.

"We weren't really in love," he said honestly, "but we had a lot in common. She loved horses, for one thing. Maybe it's crazy, but I can't imagine getting involved with a girl who didn't like to ride." He smiled.

Christie wanted to thank somebody for those wonderful words, for the luck of their meeting.

It was after midnight when they started out to his blue Mustang. Christie slid her hand through Scott's arm, needing to touch him. He smiled again.

He pulled up in front of her house and stopped the car. Her parents had left a light burning in the living room, and the small panes of glass next to the door were lit up invitingly. She sat close to Scott, and they remained silent for a while. She felt completely relaxed for the first time in weeks.

He put his arms around her and stroked her cheek with his fingertips. She snuggled closer, and he kissed her forehead gently, then raised her chin and kissed her lips. She was happy. This was what she had always hoped being in love would be like. It felt right. She sighed contentedly, her cares momentarily forgotten.

Time passed too quickly, and soon the digital clock on the dashboard read 12:31.

"I'd better go in," she said. "I don't want to, but I have to."

It was his turn to sigh. He walked her to the door and kissed her once more before they said good night. She closed the door and turned to watch him through the window as he got into his car and drove away.

It seemed so real, yet she knew it was a dream. Her feet felt icy in the wet grass, and the chilling wind whipped her thin nightgown around her body. If she could only get to the barn. Something sinister yet irresistibly sweet was waiting there. She reached out to open the gate, and the cold metal stung her flesh. Her sensations were clearer and stronger than any she had known on either side of sleep.

Somewhere a car backfired. The sharp, loud explosion woke Christie. She gasped. She was standing at the gate. It had not been a dream. She had left her bed and walked here. She was outside in the night air. And in the shadows something tempting, wondrous, and disturbing was yearning for her.

"Criosdan." The old Gaelic name was whispered with the rolled *r*'s that had begun to seem so right. In the shadows she could see the shape of a huge horse and in the saddle the bulky figure of a rider. Slowly the rider extended a long, pale hand, beckoning her to come closer. Mindlessly, she lifted a foot to start toward him.

Suddenly, Christie realized what she was doing. She cried out and whirled, afraid her house wouldn't be behind her. But it was there, square and sure, silhouetted against the sky. Christie raced to the front door, hurried up the stairs, and threw herself on her soft bed, trembling. Far away a horse neighed. She gripped the sides of her bed with both hands to keep from rising again and going to meet the strange presence that had such power over her. She began to sob. But whether her tears were because she wanted to touch that dark hand or because she feared it she did not know.

Chapter Eleven

"It's hideous! I won't wear it!"

Sue Ellen Lindsay stood in front of the full-length mirror backstage, where the members of the cast were trying on their costumes. The dress Christie had designed for her was a bold shade of red, with a low-cut neckline.

"Oh, my," said Mrs. Burnham. "Reginald Jones thought it was excellent."

"Well, I don't!" snapped Sue Ellen.

"What's wrong with it?" asked Christie. She was tired from lack of sleep and from working long hours to complete the costumes in time for the play. She wasn't up to a confontration with Sue Ellen.

"What's wrong? Dulcinea would never have worn a dress like this!"

"Sure she would have. She was sort of a tramp, and you look perfect in her dress." The actors standing nearby giggled and Christie bit her lip, regretting her words. She didn't want to fight with Sue Ellen, but she was angry and tired.

Sue Ellen stood with her hands on her hips, seething. She looked as if she could kill Christie.

"Oh, dear! Oh, my!" said Mrs. Burnham.

Christie wished Mrs. Burnham would put Sue Ellen in her place. Suddenly, Christie smelled a whiff of fresh hay, and something silver flashed, dazzling her for a second. Startled, she looked at the others. Obviously they had not smelled or seen anything. Christie panicked. Now she was having hallucinations in the daytime, too.

Mrs. Burham looked at her strangely. The teacher's face had changed. Her fluttering hands fell to her sides, and when she spoke, her accent had lost its phoniness.

"You must wear it," she said to Sue Ellen. There was steel in her voice. "Christie has worked very hard, and there is not time to make another dress. The costume has been approved by a top designer. There is nothing at all wrong with it. I know you are the star of this show, but if you insist on being unreasonable and difficult, I will give the part to your understudy."

The cast members looked at this new Mrs. Burnham, stunned. Sue Ellen's face turned red, then pale. She shot a hateful glare at Christie.

"Of course I want to play the part, Mrs. Burnham," she mumbled.

Christie felt limp. She had won. But how? How?

Christie met Scott in the cafeteria for lunch.

"Hey, you look beat," Scott said when he joined her.

"That's a great thing to tell a girl," she said wearily. "But I am tired."

"The play getting to be too much?"

"That's only part of it."

"Care to talk about what's on your mind?"

She thought a moment. It wasn't like her to complain. She had always believed that she could handle anything that came her way. But now she was beginning to wonder. Her strange dreams and Hawk's death had upset her terribly. Maybe she could talk to Scott about Sue Ellen, but she hesitated about revealing her fantasies to him. They were for her alone.

"Sue Ellen is getting on my nerves, and I guess I haven't been sleeping well."

"Because of her?"

"No. That's another problem." She sighed. "She just doesn't like me. She resents me, I guess. She thinks I deliberately tried to take Hawk away from Dee. I can't believe that could make her dislike me so much, but I don't know what else it could be."

Scott was silent for a moment. "It isn't you, Christie," he said at last. "You have a right to know what's probably behind it. It goes back a hundred years—maybe a lot longer. Your grandfather Moncrieff and Sue Ellen's grandfather Lindsay are both of Scottish descent. A long time ago back in Scotland there was apparently some kind of trouble between the Lindsays and the Moncrieffs, and they never forgot it. It seems kind of silly to hold a grudge that long, but even after members of both families came to America, the Lindsays and the Moncrieffs were never friendly. Then old Mr. Lindsay died and Sue Ellen's father took over the farm. It's a good farm. But Sue Ellen's father has a drinking problem. He got into debt and had to put the farm up for sale. Well, your grandfather bought it. He offered to let Mr. Lindsay stay on as manager, but Sue Ellen's father wouldn't hear of it. He went to work on another farm and spread rumors that your grandfather had used some sort of magic to make him lose the farm. It was crazy, of course, and nobody believed it, but Sue Ellen grew up with the story. It isn't that she hates you in particular—it's just that you're a Moncrieff. And of course your family is well off, while hers has to struggle."

Christie nodded thoughtfully. "Thanks for telling me, Scott," she said. "It does make a difference. Even so, she's been pretty mean."

Suddenly, Christie grew silent as she remembered the story she'd read in her grandfather's notebook about the hunter's wife. Was that the trouble back in Scotland that had led to this present-day feud? Was it one of Sue Ellen's ancestors who had conquered Cor Moncrieff?

Scott misunderstood her silence. He pressed her hand gently. "You'd like to be her friend, wouldn't you?" he asked. "I'll tell you what. You hang in there and let me see what I can do about Sue Ellen. We grew up together, you know. Maybe she'll listen to me."

Christie looked up and smiled. "Whatever you say," she said.

It was a relief to share at least one of her problems with Scott. Christie had been keeping things inside too long. Should she tell him about the dreams and her grandfather's notes? Her fears seemed so silly when she was with him, and besides, there wasn't anything he could do about them. She wouldn't say a word.

"The first play-off game is at home this Wednesday night against North Brighten. Can you come?"

She had forgotten that the play-offs were so near. "I'd like to. What do you think our chances are?"

"They're good. We'd have a better chance if we still had Hawk, but it should be a pretty good game anyway."

"Meet you at the gate after you win?"

He smiled at her confidence in him. "Whatever you say."

Christie worked hard, trying to finish the costumes on time. The other girls helped, and she worked at home putting the finishing touches on

Sue Ellen's dress. Sue Ellen's behavior was inexcusable. But the play was more important than a personality clash or an old feud, Christie decided.

Dee called Wednesday afternoon. Her voice had a forced cheerfulness. "Hi. Are you going to the game tonight?"

"I sure am. Are you?"

"Yeah. Why don't we go together?"

"I'd like that."

"Are you going out with Scott later?"

"Yes." Christie hoped Dee wouldn't feel left out.

"Then why don't I pick you up? I'll have my parent's car, and you won't have to worry about a ride."

The Herbert Hoover High stadium was filled. The home stands were packed with fans wearing gold and black, and the stands on the opposite side of the field were bright with North Brighten's red and blue. North Brighten had as many fans as Herbert Hoover, and they were just as loud.

The squads were already warming up on the field. Christie soon located Scott in his position as quarterback, throwing passes. It was strange not to see Hawk on the field, too, his long arms stretching out and catching those passes. Would they have a chance without him?

North Brighten kicked off, and the game began. The teams were evenly matched, and most of the battle was fought at midfield. The first score was North Brighten's, a field goal from thirty yards.

Then Herbert Hoover scored on a run up the middle by the fullback. A hole opened up for him, and he scampered fifteen yards for the touchdown.

Scott played hard and was roughed up several times, but he kept coming back, and they held the North Brighten team even until the third quarter. It was then that Jack Cole, the all-conference Herbert Hoover linebacker and fullback, was injured.

Left without one of their prime defensive men, the Herbert Hoover team tried valiantly to hold off the North Brighten attack, but gradually they crumbled before it. Christie's spirits sank. The score was 10 to 7.

Herbert Hoover went on offense, but without Hawk and the fullback, it was all up to Scott. He handed the ball off to less capable backs and threw to second-string ends who could not hold on. Their drive came to a halt, and the ball was turned over to North Brighten.

From that point on, Herbert Hoover played a defensive battle. Scott was all over the field and took a lot of punishment. It seemed to Christie that he got up more slowly after each play.

With one minute left in the game Herbert Hoover drove deep into North Brighten's territory. The home team stepped up their efforts, and their play became brutal. Scott quit throwing futile passes to ends who dropped the ball and began to carry it himself on nearly every play. North Brighten began keying on him. Christie watched anxiously, and Dee gave her hand a sympathetic squeeze, as the Trojans struggled forward, play after play, going through the middle and around the end, making useless efforts to deceive the other team with fake passes.

Then, with seconds left, Scott was thrown for a loss on North Brighten's twenty-five yard line. It was third and fifteen, and Christie knew that the only way to make up the long yardage was for Scott to throw a pass.

This was the way it had often been when Scott had thrown to Hawk to pull games out for Herbert Hoover. But there was no Hawk. Christie held her breath as Scott dropped back to throw. Neither of the receivers could get free, and he ran, was hit at the line of scrimmage, fought for two more yards, and was brought down roughly by a host of North Brighten tacklers.

Christie gasped. How could Scott survive the beating? North Brighten had won, but her only concern was Scott. She watched the players gradually disentangle themselves from the pile under which he was buried. The last man up was Scott. He was limping badly.

Dee smiled and squeezed Christie's hand again. "He's all right," she said.

Christie watched as he slowly left the field, using one of the other players as a crutch.

When Scott came through the gate, he was still limping. Christie went to him quickly.

"Oh, Scott," she said, putting her arm around his waist. "Can I help?"

"Hmmm, yes. Don't squeeze too hard, though."

She looked up, and he smiled at her.

"Did you see those guys mistreat me? If you wanted to help, you should have come out onto the field and gotten them off," he said with a low chuckle.

She beamed back at him. He was all right. Scott really was all right. She hadn't realized how much she cared for him until she thought he was hurt. She really loved him. She was filled with exhilaration just from touching him.

They went out for pizza, and he groaned as he slid into a booth. He hadn't wanted to go to Quick's, where the crowd was. He could see no reason to celebrate the loss.

They ate silently for a while. Scott's eyes were sad.

Christie asked, "Are you feeling okay?"

"We could have won with Hawk."

He said the words quietly, and Christie knew that he had not meant them selfishly. It was a statement about how much he missed his friend. Scott had not said anything while everyone else was mourning over Hawk. Yet he had been Hawk's teammate since junior high. It was always Scott and Hawk who turned losing games into victory.

Tears came to Christie's eyes. Scott had kept back his grief bravely. She reached across the table and took his hand. Pressing his fingertips to her lips, she kissed them tenderly, trying to tell him without words how much she really cared for him. His eyes told her that he felt the same way.

"If there's anything good about losing tonight, it's that I can spend more time with you now," he said. "No more practices, no more team meetings, and no more watching films for hours."

She smiled. It sounded wonderful.

"I'll finally get to meet that horse of yours. His name is Prince, isn't it? I'd like to see you ride him. Can I come over tomorrow?"

Christie smiled and nodded.

Chapter Twelve

Scott knocked on the door a few minutes after Christie got home from school the next afternoon. He was wearing a sheepskin jacket, a Stetson, and cowboy boots. He looked great, and Christie grinned as she let him in. She got her ski jacket from the hall closet.

"Mom and Dad are upstairs," she said. "I'll introduce you to them later. Care for an apple doughnut?"

"Sure."

She wrapped the doughnut in a paper towel and put it in the microwave oven to warm. While they waited, she studied him for signs of damage from the game. His face was unmarked.

"How are your ribs?"

"Better. I wouldn't want to scrimmage, but I can get around okay."

The buzzer on the microwave sounded, and Christie handed Scott the doughnut, zipped up her jacket, and headed for the door. A sudden wave of apprehension washed over her as they walked across the back yard to the gate. Heavy gray clouds filled the sky, and she shivered in the late autumn wind. She couldn't forget the night she had woken up to find herself at the gate. She tried not to remember, telling herself she had been tired and susceptible to her own imaginings. She never found anything out of the ordinary when she cared for Prince in the daylight.

Squaring her shoulders, she slid the barn door open. Prince stood quietly. Scott walked up to him and began to inspect him with an expert's eye.

"He's quite a horse," Scott said appreciatively. "It looks like he's going to turn grayer. How old did you say he is?"

"Going on three years."

Scott raised one of Prince's rear legs to inspect a hoof. Letting it fall back down, he said, "Arabians are great. We have three. If I can help you with him, let me know."

"I might take you up on that."

Prince ate his afternoon grain while she put his saddle and bridle on him. When he had finished. she led him out into the pasture, mounted him, and put him through his paces.

She rode him for about half an hour, as Scott watched. Proud of the way Prince responded, she put him through some of his more difficult maneuvers, showing off a little for Scott. Finally she rode over to Scott, and he took hold of the bridle.

"Beautiful! You're very good," he said admiringly.

"Thanks."

"What's this?" Scott asked, fingering the ornament dangling on one side of Prince's bridle.

"An old horse brass. It's from Scotland. My grandfather told me that the Moncrieffs who emigrated to American brought it over with them. My grandfather gave it to me."

"It looks so shiny and new. What kind of animal is this on it?"

Christie shivered but tried to sound casual as she replied, "Oh, some imaginary creature from folklore. It's called the Pictish Beast."

Scott hesitated. "You know, Sue Ellen likes horses. You ought to mention Prince to her, maybe offer her a ride. She might come around and say she's sorry, and you two could end the old family feud."

"It's an idea. I hate having an enemy. I wish she would make up. I have my doubts that it'll work, but I'll try to give her a chance."

She dismounted, and they led Prince back to his stall, where they removed his saddle and bridle. A thought nagged at the back of Christie's mind, but she couldn't seem to bring it forward. When they finished, they let Prince loose in the pasture and walked back to the house, their arms linked.

"Mother, this is Scott."

"Hello, Mrs. Moncrieff."

"Hi, Scott. I understand things didn't go very

well at the game last night."

"No. They sure didn't."

"Come on upstairs, Scott. I want you to meet my dad. He's in the office, isn't he, Mom?"

"Yes, I believe so."

They found her father working the computer terminal.

"Dad, this is Scott Samson."

Her father gave one last punch to the keyboard, swiveled his chair around, and stood up, holding out his hand. "Glad to know you. I've read about some of your exploits on the football field in the *Register*. You're a senior, aren't you?"

"Yes, sir."

"Have any scholarship offers?"

"Some. I'm not going to play ball in college, though. I want to spend my time on my studies. My future isn't in football. It's in agriculture."

"Oh? What school are you going to?"

"Iowa State. I want to be able to run our farm when the time comes. I've almost talked my father into getting a computer, too. What kind is that?"

Oh, no, thought Christie. I've just lost him.

A look of pride spread across her father's face as he showed Scott the computer terminal. Soon the two were engrossed in talk of computers and grain commodities, and she stood back, watching. Realizing that the best thing for her to do was to let their discussion run its course, she left them and went back downstairs.

"Where is Scott?" her mother asked.

"Captured by Dad."

"Sports or computers?"

"Computers, this time."

Her mother shook her head and chuckled.

Scott stayed for dinner, and although Christie was happy, she couldn't get rid of the feeling that she was forgetting something important. It probably has to do with the costumes, she decided. She'd recall whatever it was later. She shrugged off the uneasy feeling and focused on Scott. She made popcorn after dinner, and they talked until it was time for him to go.

"Can you sit with me at the play next Wednesday?" he asked.

"Sure. I have to be backstage before it starts in case there are any problems, but after the curtain goes up, I can come out front."

"Good. I'll save you a seat."

They stood at the door, quietly kissing and touching.

"I think I'm falling in love with you," he said.

"And I'm falling in love with you, back," Christie murmured.

Their parting kiss was lingering. Christie hated to see Scott leave.

Again she was standing before the dark, looming shape of the barn. She had been reaching out for the door handle when she suddenly woke up. The familiar terror filled her, as Christie realized she had once again walked outside in her sleep. This time she'd come even closer to the barn before waking up. Her feet were almost frozen, and she shivered violently. She spun around to leave, but an urgent yearning to stay held her.

She knew that she had to get away, but she was drawn to the barn door. What was behind it? If she opened it, what would she find? She stepped closer, raising her fingers to the handle. She wanted to go in. She wanted to know, at last, what was causing the torment in her mind. She gripped the handle, not noticing the cold of the hard metal. She wanted to be inside with Prince. She could hear his soft breathing, rhythmic and peaceful. The inside of the stall would be warm.

Suddenly, fear gripped her. What was she doing?

Summoning all her will power, she turned and ran for the safety of the house. She stumbled in the woods and fell, a branch raking across her cheek. She scrambled to her feet and ran again. The gate latch stuck momentarily, and she fumbled with it desperately. Finally it released, and she ran on, leaving the gate swinging behind her. She clawed the back door open and ran through the hall and up the stairs to her room. She turned on the light and grabbed the blankets from her bed, wrapping them around her and sitting down in the chair facing the window that overlooked the horse lot. Gradually her shivering subsided, and she sat rigidly still, staring out at the woods behind the house.

It had happened again. Each time she went a few steps farther. Each time she seemed to know more, desire more. Where would it end? If only she could understand what was mysteriously attracting her to the dark barn. She trembled. Did she really want to know?

Chapter Thirteen

Gradually the pale dawn brightened the windows of her room. Christie sat, still huddled in the blanket and staring out the window, reluctant to go back to sleep for fear that she might awaken and find herself at the barn again. Her body was stiff from the tense vigil. She had to find out what was out there in the dark, calling to her, drawing her. Was it the spirit of Cor Moncrieff, returned from the past to possess her?

Or was she going out of her mind? There was really no other explanation. Ghosts from the past simply did not appear anywhere except in the minds of the mad.

The light of day only plunged her into a deeper stupor. The morning wore on, and she remained in the chair, staring out the window. The sounds of her mother and father downstairs aroused no flicker of awareness in her eyes. At eleven o'clock her door opened, and her mother looked in.

"Oh, there you are, honey," her mother said cheerfully. "We wondered if you were sleeping late. What time did Scott leave last night, anyway?"

Christie turned her head slowly, her eyes glassy. Her mother's eyebrows drew together in concern. "Are you all right, dear?" Quickly she approached her daughter and put her hand on Christie's forehead the way she always did when she suspected Christie might be coming down with something.

Christie spoke softly. "I'm not sick."

"You don't have a fever. Did you have a fight with Scott?"

"No."

"Well, you certainly don't look well. Do you have a headache?"

Her mother's questions pulled her thoughts back from the barn, and Christie sat up straight. "I'll be all right, Mom. I've just got something on my mind."

"Can I help?"

How could Christie tell her mother that she might be going crazy? Her mother would never believe that a dead relative had come back to haunt her.

"I'll be all right."

Her mother looked at Christie for a moment and then turned to leave. "Why don't you come

118

down and have some breakfast? I think you should rest today, not even work on the costumes."

Christie had slaved away the last few days, and the costumes were almost ready. The other girls could finish the sewing, and she could check them Wednesday before the play. She needed to rest. She needed time to think, to understand what was happening to her, to decide if she needed help. She slumped deeper in the chair, exhausted. Christie Moncrieff, who had always been so proud of her independence, was admitting to herself that she might not be able to cope.

Scott called, and his voice lifted her spirits.

"Is there any reason why Prince has to be put into his stall every night?" Christie asked him.

"No, not really. People who show horses usually put them in at night to keep the animals from hurting themselves and getting marks on their coats that will cost points at a show, but most farm animals do fine if they're left outside," Scott answered. "You've seen the big bales of hay out in the fields? Farmers put them out there because they can't get their animals into the barns in the winter. Getting caught in a freezing rain is the worst thing that can happen to them."

She could leave Prince outside and pull hay out into the horse lot. That way she could avoid the barn and its frightening shadows. The solution gave her a little relief. That's what she would do.

They talked for a while longer, but Christie couldn't seem to pull herself together—even for

Scott. She just couldn't keep her mind on the conversation.

The night of the play Christie arrived at the auditorium early. She checked the actors' costumes and made sure everything was in order.

When she made a small adjustment on Sue Ellen's dress, Sue Ellen stood stiffly, her eyes on a point above Christie's head. There was a subtle change in her attitude that bewildered Christie. But there was no time to analyze it.

Christie took her seat next to Scott as the play began. She felt a sense of power and pride when Don Quixote and Sancho Panza came onstage in the costumes she had designed. The music rippled as they set out on their journey along the imaginary road that led to the inn. And there was the serving maid, the heroine of the play, Dulcinea.

But she was not wearing the red dress that Christie had designed. Sue Ellen was dressed in a low-necked, tight-waisted, full-skirted dress of bright red-and-green tartan. It didn't fit too well— it had obviously been sewn hastily from an uninspired pattern. "It's all the same to me," Dulcinea began to sing. But clearly it had not been all the same to Sue Ellen. She had to have the last word.

Scott leaned over and whispered, "That's the Lindsay tartan. Maybe she's trying to tell you that no Moncrieff is going to tell her what to wear."

Christie was furious. Her face was scarlet with anger. Sue Ellen was making a fool of her. As Dulcinea, Sue Ellen would be judged for her rich voice and her spirited acting. But Christie would be judged for that unimaginative botch of a costume.

Suddenly, time and place seemed to shift. Christie felt as though she was no longer sitting beside Scott in the school auditorium. Instead, she felt she was in the barn, reaching up to touch the ornament on Prince's bridle. "Make her sorry," she said. "Make her tell me she's sorry."

A presence radiated from the shadows, and a voice said, *"Yes, yes, lass, I will."*

"Christie!" Scott's whisper was full of concern at the strange expression on her face. "You look weird! What is it?"

"Shhh!" chided someone in back of them. Christie shook herself back to reality. She smiled brightly at Scott, nodding that everything was fine. But it wasn't. What was up on the stage wasn't fine—and neither was Christie.

She had not slept well since that last horrible night at the barn. The fear of awakening to find herself back there haunted her.

Now the clock glowed on her night table. It was three in the morning.

A faint thumping sounded in the distance. Christie listened, trying to identify it. It sounded like a horse running. She froze. Was it Prince? Or could it be Athame out there in the night?

The darkness oppressed Christie and she could not summon the courage to look out the window. Whatever it was, she did not want to know about it. She could do nothing about it. She rolled onto her side, pulled the covers over her head, and squeezed her eyes shut. Exhausted, she fell asleep.

Suddenly, the sound of horses' hooves awakened her. And a girl seemed to be sobbing, too. She thought of the story of Cor Moncrieff's nightly rides, the women he stole, and the young girls who cried in the night.

It couldn't be that. Cor Moncrieff was dead. He had been dead for two hundred years. There was no reason for him to come back.

The sounds faded, and silence hung over the house. Every fiber of Christie's body was alert. Was something going on outside?

A scream broke the silence, and someone pounded wildly on the front door.

Christie heard her father's feet hit the floor, and then the hall light flashed on. He was running down the stairs.

Christie reached for her robe and got out of bed.

Her mother was standing at the top of the stairs, looking down into the hall. Her father stood below with the door open. He was holding a hysterical Sue Ellen. She was wearing the tartan dress she had worn in the play. But it was torn and dirty. It looked as if it had been ripped by claws.

Chapter Fourteen

"Aaeeeeegh!!" The wail that rose from Sue Ellen's throat was the kind of inhuman sound that a tortured animal might make. Christie and her mother were shocked at the sight of the girl, limp in Mr. Moncrieff's arms. Sue Ellen made no effort to hold on or stand on her own feet. Her arms stuck out strangely, and her face was pale.

"Roger, what's wrong with her?" Christie's mother cried.

"She's been scared out of her wits!"

"Aaahh!" Sue Ellen continued her piteous sobbing. "Make him go away!! Make him go away!!"

Christie's mother hurried to her husband's side, and they lowered Sue Ellen to the floor.

"Get a coat from the closet!" Mrs. Moncrieff

ordered. Bending over Sue Ellen she said, "There, there, dear. Everything is going to be all right. Calm down, we're going to help you."

Christie's father folded the coat and placed it under Sue Ellen's head.

"The poor girl. What could have happened to her?" he asked.

Sue Ellen put her hands over her face, as if trying to shield her eyes from something. "Make him go away!!" she screamed.

"She must have been attacked by someone. I'll call an ambulance." Mr. Moncrieff left to call, while his wife went on trying to calm the wild-eyed girl.

Suddenly, Sue Ellen pulled her hands from her face and stared at Christie, her eyes frightened and glassy. Her voice quavered. "I'm sorry, sorry . . . "

The apology hit Christie like a blow. Suddenly, she recalled what she'd been trying to remember the day Scott was over—she'd wished Sue Ellen would make up with her. Then Christie gasped, remembering the strange sensation she'd felt at the play—she'd felt as if she were in the barn, angrily crying out to Prince that she wished Sue Ellen would apologize. Another wish had come true—and again with terrible consequences!

Christie had heard a horse galloping away, and when it returned, Sue Ellen was outside the house. Had it been Athame she'd heard? Had Cor Moncrieff fulfilled Christie's wish? Had he forced Sue Ellen to apologize?

Christie could no longer convince herself that

her imagination was simply playing tricks on her. She was certain she was the cause of what had happened to the screaming girl. Had Cor Moncrieff come out of the past because she restored the ancient amulet that linked her to him and to Athame? He had promised to give Criosdan Moncrieff anything she wished for on earth. He was honoring that promise to another Criosdan—or was it the same Criosdan? On her deathbed she had promised to go with him if he gave her—what? Christie had not made the promise. Another girl had made the vow two hundred years ago!

Sue Ellen stared at Christie. "I'm sorry," she mumbled again and again. "I'm sorry. . . . "

"Why does she keep on saying that?" Mrs. Moncrieff asked. "What does she mean? What is she sorry for?"

Christie shook her head. She could not answer. She was mesmerized by the pain in Sue Ellen's eyes. Christie could almost see the terrible image of the creature who had caused the pain. As Christie was linked with Criosdan, Sue Ellen was linked with the Lindsay wife who had ridden with Cor Moncrieff two hundred years ago. That was why Cor had seized Sue Ellen and forced her to grant Christie's wish. He did not want Sue Ellen for himself. But he had forced her to grant Criosdan's wish, just as he had forced Nell Higgins and poor Hawk to do her bidding.

"They're sending the ambulance right away," Mr. Moncrieff said. "How's she getting along?"

"I don't know," Christie's mother answered. She

looked up at Christie, sensing that her daughter had a knowledge she would not share.

Christie pulled her robe tight around her, but it didn't warm her. Her eyes locked with Sue Ellen's, each knowing what the other had seen.

The ambulance pulled away from the house, its lights flashing through the branches of the trees already bare in the face of the winter. The Moncrieffs stood at the door, watching. Two Bethel policemen waited patiently behind them, one with a notebook and a pencil in his hand. He cleared his throat to get their attention.

"Sorry, folks, but I've got to know a few things. Did you hear a car or anything else before she came to the door?"

"No, I didn't," Mr. Moncrieff responded. "Did either of you?"

"No," Christie's mother said and looked at her.

Christie hesitated before saying quietly, "No, I didn't either."

"Did she say anything that might give us a clue as to who she might have been with?"

"No, nothing," Christie's father answered. Her mother shook her head in agreement.

The policeman frowned and closed his book. "If you think of anything, please let us know. We can use any help we can get."

"We will," said her dad.

The police left, and her mother and father went into the living room and sat down.

"I'm not going to be able to sleep anymore tonight," said her mother.

Christie said good night and went up to her room.

She sat in the chair, staring at the window that overlooked the horse lot. The lamp on the table filled the room with a soft light, but Christie didn't notice it. A single thought pounded in her head. He's here, she thought. He's here.

But was she afraid—or eager?

A freak early winter storm blanketed the ground with four inches of snow by morning. It was still snowing when Scott met Christie at the front door of the school before classes started.

"I heard what happened. Who in the world could have done that to Sue Ellen? How is she, have you heard?" he asked.

"No. A helicopter took her to Mercy Hospital in Des Moines, but I haven't heard about her condition this morning." Christie avoided answering Scott's original question. She knew who had done it.

He walked her to her first class. Her classmates gathered around her and asked questions. Christie told them she didn't know anything and went quickly to her seat.

Throughout the morning everyone seemed on edge. After the third period Scott met her at her classroom door.

"I talked to Sue Ellen's brother. He said they can't make sense out of anything she says. She's been talking about a horse and rider. She keeps mumbling that she's sorry and saying, 'Make him go away.' They think she's having a nervous breakdown."

Christie stared at Scott. Was she having a breakdown too? Christie felt desperate. She couldn't keep her terrible knowledge to herself any longer.

He looked at her closely, his eyes full of concern. "Christie, what is it?"

"Can we go someplace where we can be alone?"

"Sure. Let's go to my car."

He started the engine of the Mustang and let it idle a few minutes before turning on the heater. Soon warm air fanned across Christie's feet.

He turned to face her and sat without saying a word.

She waited, gathering her nerve to tell him what she herself could hardly believe.

Finally she said, "I know what happened to Sue Ellen."

Scott raised his eyebrows. "You do?"

She nodded. "I don't know if I can expect you or anyone else to believe it, but I know what happened last night."

"Try me," he said, smiling. But the smile didn't conceal the worry in his eyes.

She straightened her shoulders and took a deep breath. "My grandfather kept a history of our family, a collection of stories handed down to him." She looked at her hands. "One of the ancestors he wrote about was named Cor Moncrieff. He lived two hundred years ago." She shuddered. "He was supposed to have been involved in the supernatural, to have practiced the black arts and ancient rituals." She looked up, embarrassed. "I know it sounds weird. I can hardly believe it myself."

Scott smiled reassuringly. "Go ahead," he said.

"Well." She hesitated, drawing another deep breath. "Cor Moncrieff had a special power. He had this horse called Athame. When Cor whispered his wishes to his horse, things would happen."

"What kind of things?"

"Just about anything, according to the legend. He could make horses die if he didn't like their owners—things like that."

"That sounds like an old wives' tale, Christie. What does it have to do with Sue Ellen?"

"Supposedly Cor Moncrieff would go out at night and bring girls back to his house. He was finally killed by an outraged husband. Before Hawk's accident, I whispered to Prince that I wished Hawk would go away. He was killed right after that."

"Hey, that's no reason—" Scott started to say.

"Wait." She put her hand on his leg. "I'm not through. That day you met Prince I said I wanted to be friends with Sue Ellen. Then, at the play, when I saw Sue Ellen in that tartan dress, something weird happened. I felt as if I'd left my body sitting in the auditorium beside you and had gone to the barn. I touched the ornament on Prince's bridle and told him I wanted Sue Ellen to apologize—it seemed so real!" Christie stopped talking for a minute, trying to slow her racing heart. "Last night after the play, I heard a horse running away from the house. Later I heard it come back. Then Sue Ellen came to the door, and my father brought her in. She was crying hysterically, but she looked at me and said she was sorry."

Scott remained silent for a moment. Christie was sure he must think she was out of her mind.

"Is there anything else that makes you think that you're being visited by this ancestor?" he asked.

"You don't believe me." She sighed. "I don't believe myself, so how can I blame you?"

"Wait a minute. I didn't say I didn't believe you. Give me a chance to absorb what you're saying. Is there anything else that makes you think this Cor Moncrieff person is behind all this?"

"Yes, there are some other things. I've found myself down by the barn three times without knowing what happened. One time I went down at night to feed Prince and woke up the next morning lying in the stall. Two other times I've gone to bed and woken up outside—once at the gate to the pasture, the other time just outside the barn. I don't know how I got there."

"Maybe you were walking in your sleep."

"Could be, but I don't think so."

"Look, Christie, Hawk's death and this thing with Sue Ellen have really upset you. Don't you think you might be overreacting?"

She looked at him and shook her head. "No. I thought it was my imagination for a long time. I refused to believe it could be anything else." She sighed. "You might as well know it all. I started having dreams about Cor Moncrieff. Terrible dreams. They seem so real."

He reached for her hand. "Hey," he said. "We'll work this out."

"Do you believe me?"

"I believe that something's got you terrified. And it's real enough to you. I won't disbelieve anything until we've had a chance to explore this together."

He squeezed her hand, and relief relaxed the tense, clenched muscles at the base of her skull. She was no longer facing this terrible thing alone. She sighed deeply. Then, leaning across the seat, she kissed him.

"I'd like to see this book of your grandfather's. How about my coming over tonight?"

"Sounds perfect."

"How about seven o'clock?"

"I'll be waiting."

When Scott arrived that evening, the snow had started again, and the temperature had dropped to an unseasonable five degrees below freezing. The wind blew the snow around in dense clouds, making it impossible to see more than a body's length ahead.

After helping him get his coat and boots off, Christie took Scott straight to the attic. Her body tensed as she looked around the cluttered room. She opened the trunk and dug into the bottom, bringing out the box that held her grandfather's notebook. Tensely, mechanically, she flipped through it until she found the part about Cor

Moncrieff. She quickly handed the notebook to Scott.

Scott read slowly, turning the pages gently to keep them intact. Finally he finished and sat back on his heels.

"That's some story," he said.

"What do you think?" Christie held her breath.

"Can't tell from this. It's like any other story that gets passed down. There's probably some truth in it and a lot of fiction."

"What about Hawk and Sue Ellen? Her name is Lindsay. You said there was an old feud. And there are the other things that have happened."

"Sweetheart, they could all have been coincidences. Lindsay isn't an unusual name. I'm not saying there's nothing to it. I just don't know that there's enough evidence to prove there's anything out of the ordinary going on. Look, I'm going down to the barn to look around."

"No!" Christie shouted, surprising herself with her forcefulness. "You can't do that. It's late. It's already dark. Don't go down there."

"Hey, look. There's not a thing down there that's going to hurt me. If what you say is true, I'll be safe as long as you don't tell Prince you want me done in. You wouldn't do that, would you," he teased.

"That's not funny, Scott," Christie said angrily.

"I'm right, though."

She surrendered. "I guess so."

They came down from the attic, and he put on his coat. "Got a pair of pliers around here?"

"Sure. There's probably a pair down in Dad's

132

toolbox on his workbench," Christie said in surprise. "Why?"

"Just had an idea. I'll explain later."

When she came up from the basement, Scott had his boots on and was pulling on his gloves. "Thanks." He took the pliers and a flashlight, gave her a quick kiss, and went out the back door. She watched from the window as he disappeared through the swirling snow into the darkness of the trees.

"He's coming."

Christie jumped. Those words! Had she imagined them? If not, who had spoken? Cor Moncrieff? But even if he was a spirit come to make his lost Criosdan's wishes come true, Cor Moncrieff would have no reason to harm Scott, thought Christie. Scott Samson had been part of no ancient quarrel. Then the memory of words she'd read in her grandfather's notebook cut her like a knife: "He pursued her and picked a fight with any young man who so much as looked at her." Cor Moncrieff did want Scott. Scott had not only looked at her, he had kissed her and won her love. She feared all the jealousy of the love-crazed highland warlock was directed against Scott.

"Closer. He's coming closer." Christie heard the voice again, rasping with evil humor. *"Let him get closer, my beauty."*

Christie faced a terrible truth about herself for the first time. In spite of her fear and remorse she had been half-proud that Cor Moncrieff served her. Now she understood what Criosdan must have known, what had made her reject Cor

133

Moncrieff until desperation in the face of death made her ask for his help. Cor Moncrieff was pure evil. He did not blindly grant Christie's wishes. He was not her instrument. He granted her wishes because they gave him the chance to hurt the young, the strong, the talented. And he punished Christie with guilt each time he made a wish come true. Now he was waiting for Scott, Christie knew. Cor and Athame were waiting in the dark for Scott to come through the woods. She had sent Scott to Cor Moncrieff! She had to stop the horror that was about to happen. She couldn't let Scott walk into Cor's trap.

She threw open the back door, shivering in her thin T-shirt, and ran out into the snow and the howling wind.

Chapter Fifteen

"Scott!" she yelled.

Off to the side she heard a noise and saw a movement. A huge shadow was weaving its way through the trees.

Christie sobbed uncontrollably as she fumbled with the latch on the gate. Finally it opened.

"He's here, my beauty." The words sounded in her brain. *"Shall we give him a proper welcome?"* Again Christie saw movement in the trees, but now the great shadow seemed to be heading in Scott's direction.

"Scott, look out!" she screamed into the biting wind. Christie ran down the path, leaving the gate swinging behind her.

Christie heard muffled drumming of hooves and the sound of breaking branches. She saw the immense shadow bearing down on the frail figure holding a flashlight. Scott turned and shone the beam of light into the trees.

Suddenly, there was a crash. The flashlight flew into the air, spinning. It landed yards away from Scott and went out. All was silent, except for the cold wind whistling through the bare branches.

Panting, Christie ran to the place where Scott had fallen. His body lay twisted between two trees at the side of the path. His breath came in heavy gasps. She reached him and pulled him onto his back.

"Oh, Scott! Are you all right?"

He moaned weakly. The sound was almost drowned out by Cor Moncrieff's demonic laughter.

Christie looked into the trees but saw nothing. She turned toward the pasture. Cor and Athame were out there, standing motionless. The falling snow made their images appear and disappear. She knew they were watching her. They were waiting. But why? She turned back to Scott.

"Can you hear me, Scott? Can you hear me?"

He moaned again and moved his head in acknowledgment.

She slid her arms under his and tugged with all her strength. He gasped. She knew he was fighting the pain. The figures still loomed like dark statues in the distance. Would Cor attack again if they tried to get out of the pasture? Would he try to kill her too?

Christie strained again to move Scott. She prayed she was strong enough to get him back up the hill and away from danger. Still Cor waited, motionless.

She pulled and pulled. Finally Scott was clear of the trees.

"Oh, please, Scott, help!" she sobbed.

She could feel him bend his knees and push with his heels, trying to help her move him. She pulled him around so that his head was pointed toward the gate. Gripping his collar, she began to pull again. Scott moved a few inches. She tugged again and moved him a little farther. The cold numbed her bare hands, and the wind chilled her through her scant clothing. There was no time to consider her own pain.

In the mist of the snow Cor Moncrieff and Athame shifted to watch Christie's painful progress. She could see the great horse's tail swish through the falling snowflakes, but no snow landed on the horse's back nor on his master's shoulders.

Desperate, Christie pulled harder. Cor might move at any second. She was too terrified even to make a sound.

She managed to move Scott a greater distance this time. Scott seemed to be gaining some mobility in his right leg, and he pushed against the ground, helping Christie to pull him forward.

"Help me up," Scott whispered.

Sobbing with relief, Christie helped him struggle to his knees.

"Come on, Scott! We can make it to the house if you'll try!"

Christie saw movement in the snow once again. Cor Moncrieff and Athame were closer now.

Would they attack and force their prey down to the frozen earth?

Scott got to his feet. Christie put her shoulder under his arm. He leaned on her, and they moved more quickly toward the gate. Was Cor riding after them? She urged Scott on, afraid to turn around.

They reached the gate, open as she had left it, and made their way into the yard. It seemed as if they were moving in slow motion. Scott was dragging one leg.

Christie chanced a look back when they reached the door. Cor Moncrieff and Athame were still standing in the pasture.

"Never fear, she will return to us," the rasping voice whispered.

Why hadn't Cor finished what he had started? It would have been so easy. He must have a reason, thought Christie. She was certain that she had something to do with that reason.

She opened the door, and took Scott inside.

Her mother and father came running, crying out in concern.

"Christie, what's wrong?" her father gasped. "What's happened to Scott?"

"Scott's hurt! Help me with him!"

"Oh, no! What happened?" asked her mother.

"Cor—" Christie broke off, realizing that she couldn't possibly tell them about Cor Moncrieff right now. "Prince spooked and ran over him." Maybe she could explain later. Maybe. But now, all that mattered was Scott.

"Let's get him into the living room and put him on the couch," said her dad.

"I'll get the first-aid kit," her mother called over her shoulder, running down the hall.

Soon Scott was lying on the couch, his shirt open, her mother studying his wounds. Christie crouched on the floor beside him.

"He's been hurt badly. I think he has some broken ribs. And look at those nasty gashes—he's been hit on the head. He may have a concussion."

"He was dragging his leg on the way up to the house," Christie told her mother. Her hands shook violently—she knew the ordeal wasn't over.

"We'll look at his leg in a moment. I want to get these head wounds taken care of first. Roger, I think you'd better call the ambulance."

"I should have done that first thing."

"Now, don't get excited, Christie. Scott will be all right." Her mother tried to sound reassuring.

But would he be all right, with Cor Moncrieff out there? Cor had killed before. He wouldn't hesitate to murder again, thought Christie.

She rose from the floor and went to the windows that faced the back yard. She pulled aside the drapes, which had been closed against the winter storm. Still Cor Moncrieff and Athame waited, motionless. They seemed to be closer than before. The light from the living room window shone through the thickening snow and glinted off something that hung from Cor's neck. The legend said that Cor Moncrieff wore a silver chain around his neck. That was it. Under it on his chest must be the hideous tattoo of the Pictish Beast. She couldn't see it, but she knew the Beast was there. Christie's blood ran cold. This ancient spirit seemed all-powerful. He could accomplish whatever he wanted. There was no way to stop him, no way to send him back to the black place he must have come from. He would not go until he had what he had come to win. Christie was caught in the clutches of an impossible, horrific, nightmare. And she couldn't wake up.

"They'll send an ambulance as soon as they can," her father said, coming back into the room.

"I hope so, dear. This boy needs help," her mother answered. "Roger, get me something to make splints with. Christie, get a sheet out of the linen closet and cut it up for bandages."

They both hurried to do as she asked. Christie was grateful for the task. She was cutting a sheet into long strips when her father came back with a slat from the bed in the spare bedroom and began to break it into pieces.

Though the redness and swelling indicated a bad sprain, Scott's leg was not broken. Two or three ribs had certainly been fractured, so they wrapped his midriff tightly in windings of cloth.

Christie sat on the floor next to Scott. She took his hand and pressed it to her cheek. Her mother smiled at her comfortingly, and her father sat down across the room. They all waited silently for the ambulance to arrive.

It won't be long now, my beauty. Then you can bring her to me. Cor Moncrieff's voice penetrated Christie's mind through the snow and the wind. He spoke to Athame, but he spoke to her too.

Chapter Sixteen

Swept by bitter, gusting winds, the snow drifted around the fences and the woodpile in the back yard. Christie stood by the window, staring at the horse and rider waiting patiently. She knew that Cor Moncrieff was biding his time, confidently awaiting the right moment. She stared out at him, and he returned her gaze. She could not see him well, but she knew what he would look like: black hair and thick eyebrows, the silver chain around his neck, and the evil tattoo of the Pictish Beast on his bare chest. Horrified, Christie realized that she had accepted it. They would meet, face to face.

Her father entered through the front door and stomped the snow off his boots. "The temperature's dropped, and the lane is covered in snow drifts. The ambulance may have trouble getting here. We've got a real Iowa blizzard out there. I haven't seen a snowplow pass in quite a while," he said worriedly.

"I hope the ambulance can make it. Scott needs professional medical care," Mrs. Moncrieff said.

With an effort Christie turned from the window and went back to sit next to Scott. Her father apparently had not seen the horse and rider. Cor must show himself only to those he wanted to see him, thought Christie. So far her parents had not interested him. But she had delivered Scott to Cor by loving and confiding in the sweet, dark-haired boy. If the monster in the snow sensed the strong bond Christie had with her parents, would he attack them too?

"I wish they'd get here," her mother said anxiously.

"I'll give them another call," her father said, going into the kitchen to use the phone.

She heard him dial. Unable to make out the muffled conversation, she turned back to Scott, who was breathing more easily now. His strength seemed to be rebuilding as it did between plays on the football field. Christie couldn't bear to think of him pitting his battered body against an opponent she feared he had no chance of defeating. He seemed at peace now, sleeping deeply. She stroked his forehead, and a tear spilled down her cheek. She felt a hand on her arm and looked up into her mother's sad eyes.

"They say they're on the way," her father told

them when he returned to the room. "They've advised the highway department that someone's been hurt. They're going to try to get a truck out here to clear the road and the lane, but they can't make any promises. I'll watch for them at the front window." He went back into the other room.

The old grandfather clock ticked monotonously, marking the passage of time. No one spoke. The cold wind howled down the chimney.

"They're coming!" her father called from the front of the house. "See the ambulance."

Christie and her mother jumped to their feet and ran to the window. Headlights moved along the blacktop. Flashing red lights blinked through the storm. The ambulance struggled through the snow. It surged forward between drifts, building up speed to ram through the next drift. But as the vehicle lurched into the lane, it spun crazily, sliding off the road and flipping over on its side.

"Oh, no!" Christie cried. Had Cor Moncrieff stopped the ambulance?

Anxiously they watched the wrecked vehicle, waiting for the driver to open the door that stuck out of the snow and emerge. But the door remained closed.

"I've got to get out there and see if I can help them," said her father. "Someone must be hurt." Quickly he pulled his boots back on, grabbed his coat and gloves, and rushed out.

Christie and her mother watched him force his way through the snow that filled the lane. The emergency lights, still flashing, made his figure seem to jump like a dancer at a macabre disco. He had to crawl along the drifts; his progress was slow and torturous. At last he reached the ambulance and pulled open the door that lay above the snow. He was hidden from their sight for a few moments but he reappeared, heading back to the house— alone.

Christie's heart sank. Help would never reach them. Cor Moncrieff had won again!

Her father came into the house, his face grim. "Two men," he said, panting. "They're both hurt, maybe dead, and I can't get them out. Get some blankets. I've got to try to keep them warm until the snowplows can get to them. I'll call the police and tell them what's happened."

Christie and her mother ran upstairs to strip the covers from the beds as he went to make the call.

When they came down the stairs, their arms loaded with blankets, he said, "The phone's out. I can't get a dial tone. We'll just have to hope the plows get here."

He headed back out into the storm, carrying the blankets. The load made his progress more difficult this time, and he had to stop frequently to rest. Christie and her mother watched him fight his way through the blizzard to the injured men. She had never thought of her father as courageous. Like Scott, he was quiet but always there when he was needed. Would Cor Moncrieff attack him? What could Christie do to protect her father?

At last her father returned. He lurched against the door and stumbled into the room.

"Roger! What's the matter?" her mother cried. She and Christie ran to him.

"Got a pain in my chest," he gasped. His face was ashen and beaded with perspiration—in spite of the cold.

Christie and Mrs. Moncrieff helped him out of his coat and into a comfortable chair. Both were terrified. What could they do? Christie hurried to make a cup of hot tea, while her mother tugged his boots off. Her father took only a few sips of the liquid, then sank back, weak and exhausted. Her mother spread a blanket over him and kissed him gently on the forehead. His eyes closed, and gradually his labored breathing became easier and more regular.

Christie watched with a heavy heart. She knew all too well who was responsible for this latest blow. Cor Moncrieff had displayed his menacing power. Now, she feared her father's life was in danger. She turned to look at Scott. The people she loved most were gathered in this room, while outside in the raging blizzard waited the evil force capable and willing to kill them all.

She moved to the window. The horse and rider were waiting.

Chapter Seventeen

The grandfather clock chimed. It was one o'clock in the morning. Christie had been standing at the window for an hour, watching. No matter how hard the snow came down or drifted, Athame and Cor remained untouched by it. They seemed to be a reflection in a mirror from another world.

Her father snored softly in his chair, his head thrown back. Her mother sat at his feet, her head on his legs. Scott was sleeping peacefully, his handsome face relaxed, the black lock of hair falling over the bandage on his forehead. Was she asleep too?

The stories from her grandfather's notebook played over and over in her head. Criosdan's deathbed promise to Cor Moncrieff burned in Christie's memory. "I will go with you if . . ."

Could her last wish have been that Cor spare someone she loved?

Christie knew what she had to do. Perhaps she had always known why Cor Moncrieff had come. There was only one way to save the people she loved.

She looked at her mother and father—together, as they had always been. They loved each other deeply. She loved them too.

Christie bent down and kissed Scott on the cheek. He smiled in his sleep. The emotions he'd aroused in her were the closest she'd ever come to experiencing what her parents shared. It was because of love that she must do what had to be done to protect them.

She went into the hall and walked to the back door. She thought of going to the closet for a coat but realized that she would not need one. She opened the door and stepped out into the raging storm. The horse and rider moved forward, poised to receive what they had come through time to take. Snow swirled around Christie as she walked toward them. The dark man swung down from the back of Athame.

She felt a surge of wild, dark emotion—forbidden passions she had never dared acknowledge before. A strange excitement stirred her. She was thrilled and terrified now that these sensations were surfacing at last.

She looked up into the dark, hypnotic eyes of Cor Moncrieff. Christie's fears dissolved.

Cor's mind penetrated hers. The silver chain around his neck gleamed as if his body was lit by an inner fire, and she could see the outline of the

Pictish Beast on his flesh under its glistening links. Cor's great shoulders were cloaked in black fur, but no snow clung to him. His sharp-toothed smile broadened. He had braved the storms of centuries for this moment.

Cor Moncrieff opened his cloak and held it wide for his Criosdan. She stood, longing to go to him—yet clinging to the life she must sacrifice. A fleeting image of Scott's face flashed before her, but still she stepped toward the dark, savage past—a past that would be her future.

Christie was entranced by the powerful figure. Inside his dark cloak was another world. She heard bloodcurdling screams. Towering fires flared and twisted. Battle-axes clanged against ancient shields. Men and women in tartans and capes of fur loomed before her. Their faces aged and turned to fleshless skulls as she watched, then freshened into pink youth again. Bagpipes screamed thousand-year-old tunes that pierced her to the heart. Stallions reared and wild animals howled, attacking with razor-sharp teeth and deadly claws. With savage grace, men danced around swords crossed on the ground—then seized them and plunged them into the bodies of their countrymen, who fell and dissolved into dust. It was ghastly. It was a dream—but it was her dream, the nightmare she had once belonged to, and belonged to now.

Suddenly the door slammed, shattering the images in Cor's cloak and breaking the trance. Christie looked toward the house in a daze. It was Scott. With an effort of his tremendous will, he had pulled himself up from the sofa—just as he had risen from countless injuries on the football field. Before him he carried a blazing wooden cross fashioned from the leftover bed slats.

Christie sobbed as she watched him approach, dragging his splinted leg as if it threatened to buckle at every step. She turned back to Cor, whose dark looming figure was but a few steps away. He seemed frozen in his tracks, transfixed by the sight of the cross. Christie felt a tearing, wrenching pain as her soul reached out to both Cor and Scott. She cried out and fell to her knees in the snow.

Scott struggled on, the burning cross held high. Twice he staggered and almost fell. But each time he caught himself and lurched on, step by step, slowly and painfully, the sweat beading on his forehead. It seemed to Christie that the world moved in slow motion and that the pain in her heart would split her in half. The cross flared in the wind, and she heard Cor hiss like a trapped animal.

Scott planted the cross in the snow and by its fiery light seemed to search the ground for something. The pliers, Christie thought wildly. He's looking for the pliers! But why? She struggled to understand, but the pain in her heart engulfed her. Suddenly Scott yelled in triumph; he turned, dragged himself over to the barn and went inside. Moments later he emerged astride Prince, his splinted leg hanging uselessly on one side.

Scott reined in near the burning cross. In the glow it cast he used the pliers to open the wire ring that had fastened the ancient horse brass to

Prince's bridle. He held up the amulet, and the Pictish Beast glinted in the light.

Christie let out a cry of mingled hope, fear, and warning as she finally realized what he meant to do.

Scott pushed the amulet between the jaws of the pliers and squeezed with all his might. The metal bent and broke in two. Again and again he mangled the fragments.

Each snap of the metal brought loud whinnies of agony from Cor's great black horse. The symbol of evil was finally crushed and distorted beyond recognition. Athame reared on his hind legs, trumpeting and snorting. The warlock struggled with him frantically and leaped astride his back. As he fought to control the steed, Cor reached down for Christie and swung her up behind him.

For the first time since she had begun to dream of the fur-clad rider, she could think with a clear mind. Now that the ancient amulet that had let Cor ride into her life was destroyed, she regained the power to choose freely. For a moment she hesitated, breathing Cor Moncrieff's musky scent, savoring the uncanny strength of his arms. Then she arched her body to escape him and leaped into the storm, falling into a drift of snow.

Cor Moncrieff howled like a wolf. Christie pulled herself out of the snowbank and ran through the blizzard toward Scott, her arms outstretched, her hair streaming in the wind.

Scott raced to meet her, urging Prince with his heel and holding the fiery cross high in one hand.

Enraged, Cor Moncrieff spurred Athame in pursuit of Christie. But the huge black beast twisted and bucked, unwilling to charge closer to the flaming cross.

Christie looked back and saw Cor's fierce dark face contorted with fury. She fought the fear that surged through her and ran on toward Scott. She held out her hand, and Scott seized it, swinging her up behind him on Prince.

"No! No! She is mine!" Cor Moncrieff raged hoarsely. He wheeled Athame around to attack them. As Scott thrust out the burning cross, the great black stallion reared back in terror.

Cor Moncrieff no longer controlled his steed. Athame snorted and whinnied in panic. The stallion's dreadful power was diminishing.

A gust of wind sent the flames flaring even closer, and the black horse could bear no more. Trumpeting fearfully, he twisted away and plunged off into the darkness, his rider bellowing and cursing through the storm. Raising the fiery cross above his head, Scott hurled it after them. A fiendish shriek split the air as it struck Cor Moncrieff in the back. Flames shot upward as his fur cloak caught fire. Was he an earthly being after all, despite the passage of centuries? Or were those the consuming flames of the black abyss from which he had come?

The black steed and burning rider galloped wildly out of the horse lot, across the field, and up toward the ridge beyond, disappearing at last into the darkness with a final flash of light.

The wild, savage Scotsman had stirred her blood and awakened the memories of centuries. Her arms tightened around Scott's strong body and she pressed her half-frozen cheek to his back. This was her true love, whose life she would share from tonight on. She dismissed any regret she felt at losing her connection with the tempting past.

"Oh, Scott, I love you. I love you," she murmured softly.

The lighted windows of the farmhouse gleamed like a welcoming beacon in the darkness. As the pair made their way to the warm refuge, the faint hum of an engine reached their ears. They could see the flashing lights of a snowplow in the distance.

Scott had saved Christie from the voices in the dark. The danger was over.

As she gazed at Scott with love and gratitude, she knew her choice to be with him was right, but she would never forget those moments wrapped in Cor Moncrieff's dark cloak and the glimpse she had had of the eternal past. She had chosen freely and wisely, but she understood temptation. This sweet, earthly love would have to be enough.

Experience these other exciting TWILIGHT novels of supernatural suspense!

THE INITIATION, Robert Brunn

Something is wrong at Blair Prep. Are the strange disappearances and gruesome deaths linked to the elite club on campus? Adam and Loren are determined to uncover the dark mysteries that fester behind Blair's proper facade. But will they pay for their curiosity with an invitation to living death?

DEADLY SLEEP, Dale Cowan

Jaynie's summer vacation in Scotland hasn't been the rest she'd hoped for. Each night, she's awakened by a haunting voice that pulls her deeper and deeper into a centuries-old vendetta. Slowly, Jaynie is becoming possessed by an evil force she can't resist.

BLINK OF THE MIND, Dorothy Brenner Francis

Acts of ungodly evil have been occurring miles from the cruise ship on which Kelly and her younger sister are vacationing. Yet Kelly is able to _see_ them; she seems to possess a "sixth sense" she hardly understands. Now she's in danger and must learn to protect herself before _she_ becomes an unwitting victim of her own embryonic gift.

FATAL ATTRACTION, Imogen Howe

Janet knew that her whole world was being destroyed. Infected by someone or some_thing_ that reeked of death and decay. There _was_ something about Mirella, something about her cloying sweetness, that hid an awful evil. But who would believe Janet anyway?

THE POWER, Betsy Haynes

Someone is trying to control Meredith's mind and she's terrified. At first she thinks it's a sick joke, but gradually she feels the vise being tightened. Then, when Missy's body is found and Liz disappears, Meredith realizes she's next! Can she free herself from the killer's hypnotic commands and save her own life?